Claudia Talks About:
Skipping School

Band X is my favorite group in the whole world, and they're playing here in San Francisco this weekend! I'll do anything—*anything* to see them. Even if it means cutting classes—and making my family really angry with me.

My name is Claudia Salinger. You've probably heard about my family. Everyone at school knows the story. We live alone in my house—just my brothers, my sister, and I.

My parents died in a car accident two years ago, when I was ten. That's when my oldest brother, Charlie, became our legal guardian. He's twenty-five, so I guess everyone figured he was old enough to take care of us. But sometimes he really messes things up. Like the time he forgot to pay the electric bill. We lived in the dark for a week!

But it's okay when Charlie makes a mistake. Bailey is always there to fix it. He's my other big brother. He's in college, and he's the coolest. Whenever I have a problem, I ask Bailey for help. Like when I'm afraid I might forget how my parents' voices sounded. Or how they looked. Bailey says my brothers and sister will always be there to help me remember.

My sister, Julia, reminds me of my mother sometimes. She's really smart and pretty, like Mom was. Julia is in high school. I want to be just like her when I'm seventeen!

Then there's Owen. He's only two and a half. But I can tell that someday he's going to be a brain surgeon or something. He already knows how to spell my name with his blocks. He's *so* smart. I think he takes after me!

My brothers and sister are always busy with school or work or girlfriends and boyfriends. And I'm always busy practicing my violin. I love playing—it reminds me of my mom. Charlie says I inherited her talent. Mom used to play with one of the best orchestras in the country. Maybe one day, I'll do the same thing.

Sometimes we get so busy that we don't see one another enough. That's why we eat dinner together at least once a week. We go to Salinger's, the restaurant my dad used to own. They always have our table reserved—for a party of five.

Claudia

PARTY OF FIVE™: Claudia

Welcome to My World
Too Cool for School

Available from MINSTREL Books

party of five™

Claudia

Too Cool for School

Debra Mostow Zakarin

**Based on the television series
created by Christopher Keyser
& Amy Lippman.**

A
MINSTREL®
BOOK

Published by POCKET BOOKS
New York London Toronto Sydney Tokyo Singapore

A MINSTREL PAPERBACK *Original*

 A Minstrel Book published by
POCKET BOOKS, a division of Simon & Schuster Inc.
1230 Avenue of the Americas, New York, NY 10020

A PARACHUTE PRESS BOOK

ISBN: 0-671-00677-0

First Minstrel Books printing March 1997

10 9 8 7 6 5 4 3

Too Cool for School

chapter one

... **Y**ou're listening to the way cool sounds of San Francisco's own KZAK! This is Danny Rose, and the time is six fifty-seven A.M. . . . Time for the number three song . . ."

I didn't open my eyes as I fumbled for the snooze button on my clock radio.

". . . On the top-forty chart, 'Don't Lose It' by that sizzling hot rock group, Band X!"

I stopped fumbling and flopped back on my pillow. Band X was my favorite group in the world! And "Don't Lose It" was my favorite Band X song. What a great way to start the day.

"Claudia!" my brother Bailey called.

I ignored him. The song was just coming to my favorite

1

part—where the Band X violinist, Jam, saws out this weird, whiny solo. I didn't want to miss it.

"Claudia!" Bailey yelled again. He pushed open my door and stuck his head inside.

"What?" I mumbled. Now I totally missed Jam's solo. Brothers can be such a pain.

"Have you seen my green polo shirt?" he asked.

"Not since you had it on last night at dinner," I answered. "Maybe you left it in your apartment."

"No, all my laundry is here—there's, like, nothing left in my apartment," he said. "That was my only semi-clean shirt, and now it's gone. Somebody took it!"

"Not guilty," I said. "I wouldn't even *want* your shirt."

"Julia better do some laundry, and I mean soon," Bailey said. "I need something to wear to dinner with Sarah tonight."

Sarah is Bailey's girlfriend. I like her. But that didn't mean I knew where Bailey's shirt was. "Check in the living room," I suggested.

Bailey's face vanished from my doorway, and I heard him pounding down the stairs. I smiled. It was kind of nice having Bailey barge into my room in the morning, even if he did make me miss a Band X song.

Bailey just started college. Until last month, he lived at home. But now he has an apartment across town, near his school. I don't know why he bothers paying rent, though—he's here practically every day.

I climbed out of bed. The one *really* cool thing about Bailey moving out was that I got my own room. Before, Bailey slept in the attic bedroom. And I lived in the dining room—in a tent!

I mean, I used to share a room with my sister, Julia. (She's seventeen—four and a half years older than me.) I didn't mind sharing the room. But Julia hated it. She went through some major changes two years ago, after our parents died in a car accident. Well, of course, all five of us kids did. It was the most awful time in our lives. But Julia acted the worst. She basically kicked me out of our room. She said she needed total privacy. Period.

So I slept in a tent set up in our dining room. It wasn't bad—in fact, I kind of liked it. But now that Bailey was gone, Julia had the attic room, and I had her room.

The tent was pretty cool. But it was nice to have an actual door again. And an actual bed.

"It's a beautiful Tuesday morning, and the time is seven o'clock," Danny Rose announced from the radio. I turned it off and headed for the bathroom to brush my teeth.

As soon as I stepped into the hallway, I bumped into my oldest brother, Charlie. He was carrying my *youngest* brother, Owen, who's two and a half.

Charlie is twenty-five. He's the oldest Salinger kid, and he was appointed the legal guardian for the rest of us after our parents died. He used to be a carpenter and house-painter. He had his own apartment. But after he became our guardian, he moved back home. Now he manages Salinger's, the restaurant our dad used to own.

I studied Charlie's face. His eyes were red and he looked like he needed a shave. He puts in some pretty late nights at the restaurant.

"Morning, Claud." Charlie yawned. "I have to run down to the basement and see if I can find a clean pair of jeans," he said. "Watch Owen for a few minutes, will you?"

"Sure," I said, taking Owen from him.

"Cla-dee!" Owen squealed, opening his blue eyes wide and grinning. He wrapped his pudgy arms around my neck. His light-brown hair felt sticky as he pressed his head against my cheek.

"Come on, Owen." I turned back into my room and headed for my closet. "Help me figure out what to wear to school."

"Owen go kool," Owen crooned.

"That's right," I answered. "Owen goes to school."

Well, *school* was stretching it. Charlie took Owen to day care every morning at nine o'clock. But Owen liked to call it school. I guess he wanted to be just like the rest of us.

I opened my closet. I stared in at . . . empty hangers. I'm not into clothes the way some of my friends are. I don't have an outfit for every day of the month. But all I saw today was a pair of denim overalls I got when I was in sixth grade. Unfortunately, they still fit me (I haven't grown much since then). But they were way too babyish and out of style to wear to eighth grade at Walt Whitman Junior High.

"Uh-oh," I said.

"Uh-oh," Owen echoed.

"This is bad," I told Owen.

"Bad," he agreed.

I sighed. "All my *real* clothes are dirty. I guess I'll wear the overalls." I slid them off the hanger, and plucked a flowered turtleneck off the shelf. "Okay, Owen. Let's go brush our teeth."

"Teef!" Owen squealed with delight. If there's one thing Owen loves, it's squashing a tube of toothpaste.

We headed for the bathroom as Charlie came up from the basement.

"Teef!" Owen announced.

"That's great, Owen," Charlie said. Then he turned to me. "Whose turn is it to do laundry, anyway? Bailey's or Julia's?"

I shrugged. "Bailey thinks it's Julia's and—"

"It's *not,*" Julia exclaimed as she came barreling down the stairs from her attic room. "I switched with Bailey two weeks ago. He just keeps forgetting it's his turn because he's not living here anymore." She stopped at the bottom of the stairs to kiss Owen.

At first when we were on our own, our house was a disaster. Then the five of us divided up the work. Well, four of us—Owen's not too big on chores yet. Charlie earns the money managing the restaurant. He's also in charge of groceries. I baby-sit for Owen three days a week after school. Bailey and Julia are in charge of everybody's laundry—washing, drying, folding, and putting it away. Bailey does it one week. Julia does it the next. At least that's the way it's *supposed* to work.

But since Bailey moved out, he just waits until everything he owns is dirty. *Then* he brings it over to wash.

"Julia, you and Bailey get this thing figured out," Charlie ordered as he passed her and headed for his room. "I have enough on my mind without worrying about the laundry."

Julia made a face at Charlie's back. Then she turned to me. "Boy, what's eating him?"

"Gee, I don't know," I said sarcastically. "Could it be he doesn't have any clean pants to wear to work?"

Julia sighed. "It's not my fault Bailey can't remember his turn. I have a million other things to worry about."

"Tell me about it," I put in quickly. "I have this huge biology test on Friday, and—"

"Teef!" Owen shrieked. "Teef!"

"Right," I agreed. "Teef." I carried him to the bathroom. Ten minutes later, Owen's teeth were brushed and I was dressed in my overalls and flowered turtleneck. Just in case I looked too babyish, I brushed my shoulder-length brown hair toward my face—the way Julia does. If I looked like Julia, that must mean I looked older, right? I even put on a little bit of Julia's makeup. She has dark brown eyes like mine, so I figured her mascara would be okay on me, too. At least, it would be okay as long as Julia didn't find out. She hates when I use her things.

After a last check in the mirror, I carried Owen down to the kitchen. Everybody else was already there. Bailey leaned on the counter, wolfing down a bowl of cereal. Julia stood staring into the open refrigerator. Charlie sat at the table, reading the paper and sipping coffee. KZAK was blaring out another great Band X song, "Ghost Rain."

"He's brushed his teef and he's all yours, Charlie," I said as I plopped Owen into his high chair.

"Booful teef!" Owen crowed.

"Beautiful!" Charlie told Owen. "Thanks, Claud," he added.

"You guys?" I asked everybody as I took a Pop-Tart out of the cabinet. "Does my outfit look totally geeky?"

Julia glanced over her shoulder. "It's fine," she told me.

I turned to Bailey. "Truth, Bay," I said, spinning around to give him the full view. "How bad is it?"

"You look great, Claud," Bailey said. "At least you have *some* clean clothes." His eyes darted to Julia.

"Don't start with me, Bay." Julia grabbed a yogurt from the fridge and shut the door—hard. "I'm down to my last two T-shirts."

"Well, I did a load over the weekend," Bailey began.

7

"Yeah, a load of *your* dirty clothes," Julia cut in.

I picked up my Pop-Tart.

"See you, guys!" I called. Then I ran up to my room, grabbed my backpack and my violin, and headed out the front door to catch the school bus.

I was running late, so I hurried down the hill. San Francisco is *filled* with hills. You get used to running up and down all the time.

The bus pulled up just as I reached the stop.

I followed Sari onto the bus. She lives three houses away from me. I used to sit with Sari on the school bus every day. Or with my friend Jeff Bloch. But now I sit with my best friend, Jody Lynch. I scanned the seats for her. With her red hair and green eyes, Jody is hard to miss. I spotted her in the backseat and made my way there, stepping over everyone's books and legs.

"Hey." I plopped my backpack down on the floor of the bus.

"Hey yourself, Fiddle Girl." Jody smiled as she made room for me on the seat beside her.

"Cut the fiddle girl, will you?" I muttered, sitting down.

"It's a compliment!" Jody grinned. "No one else has the talent to earn the title."

Jody always calls me Fiddle Girl because wherever I go, I always take along my violin. It's a really good one—worth a lot of money. But that's not why I carry it around all the time. I like to have it with me so that if the mood strikes, I can take it out and start playing.

My mother was a professional violin player. People say I inherited her talent. I keep a concert picture of my mom tucked inside my violin case. This way, I get to see her every day.

"Whoa—Claudia . . ." Jody was squinting at me with an odd expression on her face. "What's going on?"

"What?" I asked. "Why are you looking at me that way?"

"Hello? Like, what are you wearing?"

"Oh, yeah . . . well, these overalls are my last clean clothes." I sighed. "See, Bailey and Julia are having this laundry war. They've switched turns so many times they don't remember whose turn it is anymore. So, because of their immaturity, *I* have to suffer."

"Why suffer?" Jody asked. "Don't you know how to use a washing machine?"

I rolled my eyes.

"Seriously," Jody went on. "Why don't you just pick out your dirty clothes from the hamper and do your own laundry?"

"Well, sure, I could," I replied. "But why should I? I have tons of chores already. It's their responsibility."

Jody shrugged. "Just a suggestion," she said. "I can't remember the last time my mom did my laundry for me."

Jody's parents are divorced and she lives with her mom. Her dad lives in San Francisco, too, but Jody doesn't see him much. Jody's mom basically lets Jody do whatever she wants. That may sound pretty good. But I don't think Mrs. Lynch acts like much of a mom. Like never cooking dinner, or never doing Jody's laundry.

I remember when I was little, I used to sit on the dryer down in our basement. I would play scales on my violin while my mother did our laundry. Sometimes Mom would stop what she was doing and listen to me play. She would smile, and then go back to sorting the clothes. Maybe that's why I don't mind practicing scales. And—maybe I wouldn't mind doing some laundry, either. I like doing things that make me feel close to my mom.

Jody's voice broke into my thoughts. "Hey, Fiddle Girl, I've got a great idea for today."

"Yeah? Tell."

She leaned over and whispered, "Let's go to the Coffee Shop after second period."

"Yeah, right." I laughed. "I think we still have classes after second period, Jody."

Jody rolled her eyes. *"Duh,"* she said. "I mean, let's *ditch* school!"

chapter two

"Cut class?" I exclaimed.

Jody nodded.

"And go to the Coffee Shop?"

Jody nodded again.

I knew about the Coffee Shop from Bailey and Julia. It was this hip high school hangout that served all kinds of fancy coffees.

"Why do you want to go there?" I asked her.

"Because . . . I happen to know some cute high school boys who hang there," Jody answered. "Like *Troy.*"

"Give me a break." I sighed. "I'm supposed to miss class so I can hang out with some guy named Troy?" I shook my head. "I don't think so."

"Troy is way cool, Claud," Jody went on. "I know he'll

be there. I really want you to see him! I want to know what you think of him."

I groaned. Sometimes Jody goes a little nuts about boys, and it gets to me after a while. It's not that I don't like boys. Believe me—I do! But I guess having three brothers sort of takes the mystery out of boys. Jody is an only child, so she doesn't get it.

There *is* this one boy in my history class, Pete Hennesey, who's great looking. He has red hair and cute dimples when he smiles. I really like him, but I haven't ever told anyone. Well, except Jody.

"Oh, come on, Claudia," Jody was saying. "You and me. It'll be fun! You'll love the Coffee Shop."

"You come on," I said. "I mean, I don't even drink coffee."

"So? Big deal. You can get a latte. Or a frappe. Even a hot chocolate."

"Forget coffee for a second," I told her. "I can't just 'ditch school.' I mean, what if we get caught?"

"Trust me," Jody said with a knowing look. "We won't get caught."

I wanted to trust Jody. After all, she *was* my best friend. But Jody does a lot of outrageous things. Sometimes she gets away with them. But other times, she gets caught. She's practically famous for cutting classes. She has a pretty bad reputation. Even Charlie has heard things about her. He's not exactly thrilled that I've picked her as my best friend.

But people don't know the *real* Jody. She's totally loyal. Plus she's so much fun. I've had the best times of my whole life with her.

The last thing in the world I wanted was for Jody to think I wasn't cool enough to hang out with her. But still—I had to tell her what was bothering me.

"I know it sounds nerdy and everything," I began, "but I don't want to get into trouble."

"Believe me, Claud, getting into trouble is no fun," Jody said. "I know that better than anybody. But you *won't* get in trouble. I promise."

I didn't know what to say. How could she be so sure?

"Come on, Claud," Jody urged. "You need some fun in your life. Walk on the wild side for a change!"

"Well . . . getting in trouble isn't the only thing," I argued. "I hate it when I miss stuff in class and get all confused, and I have this big biology test on Friday—"

"Claud, this is Tuesday," Jody cut in. "Friday is like a million hours away."

"I know," I said. "But Mr. Grodinski is reviewing all week. I just can't miss science."

"What period do you have it?" Jody asked.

"Seventh," I told her.

"Perfect!" Jody exclaimed. "We'll cut out second period

and come back to school during fourth period lunch. Nobody will catch us, and you'll be there for the bio review."

I thought for a moment. She definitely had a point. "Yeah, well, that might work. . . ."

"Please!" Jody stared at me with those big green eyes of hers. "Pretty please! I'll be your best friend."

I giggled. "You already *are* my best friend," I pointed out.

"Then come to the Coffee Shop with me," Jody insisted.

"Well—okay," I said at last. "Why not?" Maybe it would even be fun.

"That's the way, Fiddle Girl!" Jody slapped me on the back.

I felt pretty proud of myself for having the guts to cut. Jody was right. I was always studying or practicing my violin—boring stuff. I *needed* some fun in my life.

"Let's meet at nine-thirty," Jody said.

"But that's right in the middle of second period," I protested.

"No kidding." Jody grinned.

"Well, how am I supposed to get out of class right in the middle?" I cried. "I thought we were going to skip the whole period."

Jody rolled her eyes. "Claudia, please. Just trust me a little bit," she said. "If you leave in the middle of a class, it's less obvious that you're actually cutting it."

"Why?"

"Think about it," Jody said. "Most kids cut a *whole* class—they just never show up, and the teachers know they're cutting. That's why they get caught. Right?"

"I guess," I said.

"But *we* will go to class, so the teachers know we didn't cut. And then we'll make up excuses to leave in the middle—with the teacher's permission! They'll never guess that we really just cut out. Get it?"

She was right! How could I get in trouble for cutting if the teacher *knew* I was leaving? I bet that doesn't even really count as cutting class.

I nodded. "I have math second period. You have French, right?"

"Right," Jody said.

"So, where should we meet?" I asked.

"In the third-floor girls' bathroom," Jody whispered. "The first one there should go into the fourth stall."

"Okay," I whispered back as the bus pulled up in front of Walt Whitman Junior High School. "See you!"

"Nine-thirty sharp, Claud," Jody reminded me. "And don't flake out on me."

"Please," I told her as I picked up my backpack and my violin case. "Have some faith."

Jody and I were swept up into the crowd as we walked through the double doors into school. My heart beat with excitement. I glanced at my watch. In less than two hours, I'd be cutting school for the first time ever!

I headed for my first period class, social studies. Most mornings, I like that class. We were studying the American Revolution, and Mr. Chandler always made it seem pretty interesting. But that morning, I barely heard a word my teacher said. I just sat at my desk, staring at the big wall clock over his head. I watched it slowly ticking the minutes away.

"Claudia?" someone whispered.

I turned toward the desk next to mine. Pete Hennesey's desk!

"Um . . . Claudia?" Pete said again.

"Yeah?" I felt my face getting warm.

"Do you have an extra pen I could borrow?" he asked.

"Oh, sure." My face was turning hotter by the minute as I fumbled in my backpack. Who said having three brothers took the mystery out of boys?

Where was a pen? I always had plenty of pens. Pens from the restaurant. Pens that said "Salinger's" on them. So why couldn't I find one?

At last my fingers brushed against a pen. I pulled it out and handed it to Pete.

"Thanks," Pete whispered. "I'll give it back to you tomorrow."

"That's okay," I said. "Keep it. We have millions of them. Well, hundreds anyway."

Pete laughed. Then he bent over his paper and started taking notes. I watched him to make sure the pen actually *worked.*

Finally social studies ended. I pushed my way through the crowded halls to my math class. Math is my favorite subject, but no way could I concentrate on what Ms. Holtz was saying about fractions today!

Maybe I'll write a note to Jeff, I thought. He sits three desks away from me. But Jeff *hates* math—he has to concentrate really hard just to understand it. I better not bother him, I decided.

Instead, I used my time thinking up excuses for getting out of class—without being too obvious. I opened up my notebook and found a clean page. At the top I wrote *Escape Plans*. Then I wrote down some of my ideas:

1. I forgot my lunch at home and I have to go and get it.

No, I thought. That sounds like too much of a lie.

2. I offer to get bagels and coffee for the whole class at the Coffee Shop.

Yeah, like that would ever work.

3. I have a dentist appointment.

Okay, this could work. But what if Ms. Holtz asks for a note? Come on, Claudia, think!

4. I have to go to the nurse's office.

That's it! I'll tell Ms. Holtz that I have a stomachache and need to see the nurse! She'll never check with Ms. Newberger (that's our school nurse). And even if she does, Ms. Newberger is so out of it she won't remember if I was in her office or not!

I remember Julia telling me that when she was in junior high, she asked Ms. Newberger for a note every day excusing her from gym. Julia gave her the same excuse every time—that she had cramps. And it worked every single day for two whole months!

Now I felt confident. Asking to see the nurse was the perfect excuse. If it worked for Julia, it would definitely work for me.

Ms. Holtz finished explaining about fractions. She wrote ten problems on the board and then walked to her desk and sat down. I glanced up at the clock. It was nine twenty-five—time for my Academy Award-winning performance. I got up and walked up to Ms. Holtz's desk. I made sure to clutch my stomach as I walked.

Ms. Holtz looked up at me. "Yes, Claudia?" she said.

"Can I go to the nurse?" I asked. I tried to fill my voice with pain and suffering. I made tears come to my eyes.

"Is everything okay?"

"I think I ate something weird last night," I lied. "I feel sort of sick to my stomach."

"Yes, go right ahead," Ms. Holtz said quickly. I mean, what teacher in her right mind would keep a student with an upset stomach in her classroom? She probably thought I would throw up or something. I bit back a smile. Jody was right. I was having fun already!

"I hope you feel better, Claudia," Ms. Holtz said as she

18

scribbled out a hall pass for me. "Call someone in the class tonight and get the answers to these problems."

I nodded, trying to look sick. "Thank you, Ms. Holtz," I croaked. I shuffled back to my desk and stuffed my notebook into my backpack. Then I picked up my violin case and walked out of the room.

It was quiet in the long, empty hallway. As I walked toward my locker, I thought how easy it had been to get out of class. I knew Ms. Holtz didn't think I was faking. Besides, I've never skipped class before in my life. No way would Ms. Holtz suspect *me* of cutting!

When I reached my locker, I began twirling the combination lock. Twenty-three right. Twenty-nine left. Back to sixteen. And . . . my locker didn't open. I glanced around. I was the only one in the hallway. My heart began to beat hard as I tried my combination again.

What if it didn't open? Jody would think I was a total loser if I showed up to go to the Coffee Shop with my backpack and violin case!

Click! The locker door swung open. Whew!

I grabbed some money out of my backpack and tucked it into the pocket of my overalls, along with my hall pass. Then I shoved my backpack and violin case into my locker. I closed the door. I tried to do it quietly, but the sound of the metal latch catching seemed to echo through the hallway.

I checked around again. No one was coming. So I headed for the stairs at the end of the hall.

I climbed quickly to the third floor and walked down another long, silent hallway. It was weird to pass the classroom doors and see all those kids sitting at their desks. They're all trapped in their classes, I thought. And *I'm* not!

I checked my watch. Nine thirty-five. Uh-oh! Jody would have gotten to the bathroom five minutes ago!

I hurried down the hall. I didn't want Jody to be mad at me for showing up late. I pushed open the door to the girls' bathroom and walked into the big gray-and-yellow tiled space. It was totally quiet.

I counted the gray metal stall doors as I passed. One . . . two . . . three . . . four. This was it. I glanced under the door. I didn't see any feet on the floor. Maybe Jody was hiding—sitting on the toilet, with her feet pulled up. The door was slightly open.

"Jody?" I whispered.

She didn't answer.

I pushed the door open.

I stared at the toilet.

Jody wasn't there.

chapter three

I thought time crawled when I was watching the clock in social studies. But that was nothing. As I sat on the toilet in the fourth stall of the third-floor girls' room, time seemed to practically stop.

Where was Jody? Was she coming? Had she gotten caught? Or had she been here at nine-thirty?

Maybe she left because I was late. She probably figured I chickened out!

No way, I told myself. She would have waited for five minutes. But then—where was she? I felt like a jerk, sitting there. What if a teacher came in?

Okay, Claudia, take some deep breaths. I tried to calm myself down, the way I do before I play a piece on my violin.

If a teacher came in, I could say I was on my way to the nurse but I didn't feel good, so I stopped off in the bathroom.

I would just have to hope the teacher didn't ask why I climbed two flights of stairs to come to the third-floor girls' room!

I took a few more deep breaths. Then I made my plan. If Jody wasn't there by nine forty-five, I'd go down to the nurse's office and follow through with the upset stomach plan.

I half wished I had my biology book with me so I could get in some studying. But I didn't. So I did the only thing you can do when you're stuck in a toilet stall—I read the walls.

I found out a lot of stuff. Like, Halle loves Adam. Brian and Laurie are together forever. If you want to have a good time call Kenny at home after eight o'clock. And, oh yeah, school stinks.

No, I'll tell you what stinks. Being stranded in a toilet stall waiting for your best friend to show up—that stinks!

I was mad now. It was nine forty-five—and no Jody. That's it, I decided. I'm out of here. Getting out of class had been sort of fun. But sitting on a toilet waiting wasn't. I pushed open the stall door and stepped out.

Jody was leaning against the wall across from the fourth stall—as if *she'd* been waiting for *me!* "Hey, Fiddle Girl," she said. "What's happening?"

"Jody!" I exclaimed. "I've been waiting in there forever. Where have you been?"

"What do you mean?" she asked innocently. "I'm here."

"Well, you weren't here at nine thirty-five," I pointed out angrily. "I was about to go to the nurse's office for real."

Jody shrugged. "Sorry, Claud. I figured that since this was your first time getting out of class, it would take you a while."

"Well, then I guess you didn't figure that I'd be a natural at it," I told her.

"Yeah?" Jody grinned.

"Yeah," I said, grinning back. I forgot all about being angry. "I was amazing, Jody! I told Ms. Holtz I was sick, and I made myself sound weak and sad, like I was really about to puke. I think I should be an actress."

Jody laughed. "I'm proud of you!" She put an arm around my shoulder. "Come on, Claud," she said. "I'll buy you a hot chocolate."

"And a donut?" I asked as we headed out of the girls' room.

"Wow. You're really pushing it. Okay, and a donut," Jody promised. "So, are you still mad at me for being late?"

"I'll let you know *after* I've finished my donut and hot chocolate," I joked.

Okay, so I'm a sucker for my best friend. And for hot chocolate. I really wasn't angry anymore. I was having fun again. It felt cool being in the hallway with Jody, knowing that everyone else was still in class.

We snuck down the stairs to the ground floor. There's a door at the base of the stairwell. But at the bottom of the steps stood a short girl with blond, curly hair and granny glasses.

"Uh . . . hi," I muttered as we started to walk past her.

"Hold it a minute. I'm the first-floor hall monitor," the girl told us. "Where are your hall passes?"

"Who wants to know?" Jody asked in a snotty voice.

I shot Jody a look. Now was *not* the time to get on the bad side of the hall monitor.

"I do," the blond girl answered. She clicked her retainer with her tongue.

Jody folded her arms across her chest.

But before she could open her mouth and get us into some *real* trouble, I opened mine.

"We just got excused from class," I said in my "sick" voice. "Ms. Holtz asked my friend to take me down to the nurse's office. I'm really sick to my stomach. But—" I fumbled in the pocket of my overalls. "Here's my pass."

I handed it to her.

Out of the corner of my eye I saw Jody grin.

"The teacher didn't have time to give us both a pass," Jody put in, picking up on my story. "And my friend is going to barf any second!"

"Okay," the monitor said. "Go on."

I tried to look sick as Jody and I started back down the hallway.

"Don't turn around," Jody whispered. "She's watching us."

"How do you know?" I whispered back.

"Experience," Jody said. "Once we get around the corner, we'll be okay. That girl's a new hall monitor. Believe me—I know all the regulars. She won't leave her post by the stairs."

We kept walking until we turned the corner. Then we broke into a run, aiming for a different back door.

When we got to the exit, Jody reached out with both hands and pushed the long metal bar that ran across the door. It swung open. I half expected an alarm bell to start ringing.

We ran outside. The cool air hit my face and I breathed deeply. I never realized just how stuffy school was until I had a little breath of freedom!

I didn't have much time for breathing, though. Jody grabbed my hand and pulled me toward the teachers' parking lot. We ran between parked cars, heading for the football field.

Once we got to the football field, Jody let go of my hand. She ran ahead of me. I had a hard time keeping up with her.

"Slow down," I shouted in a hoarse whisper.

"No, come on," Jody insisted. "We're almost there."

"There?" I called. "Where's there?"

"You'll see," Jody said. "Just come on!"

We ran across the football field and then over some grass to a tall, chain-link fence. When we got there, Jody walked over to a section where the bottom of the fence had been bent up a bit. The grass beneath it was worn away.

"Crawl under," Jody said.

"You must be joking!" I cried. "Through there?"

"Yeah," Jody said. "Do it!"

"Jody!" I exclaimed. "You expect me to crawl under this fence like . . . like a dog?"

Jody laughed as she picked up the bottom of the fence and held it up for me. "Get going, Rover!" she said. "Everybody else does this."

"Okay," I said. I dropped to my hands and knees and started crawling under the gap in the fence. I had to practically lie down on my stomach to fit under the wires.

"I can't believe I'm getting dirt all over my only clean clothes," I said. But I couldn't help giggling.

Finally I managed to make it through to the other side. I stood up and brushed the mud off the knees of my overalls. Then I held up the bottom of the fence. Jody hit the ground and quickly crawled through. She looked like she'd done it a million times before.

On the other side of the fence, we started running again. We cut through some backyards and finally came out along a side street. I had no idea where we were. But obviously Jody did.

I followed her, and by the time we reached the Coffee Shop, we were both panting.

We stood outside for a moment, catching our breath. Then Jody and I walked through the door.

Good smells hit me the minute I was inside the Coffee

Shop. The smell of coffee, of course, and cinnamon and chocolate. All around the sides of the room were couches and easy chairs and old coffee tables strewn with newspapers. Jody and I wound our way around small tables with wooden chairs that didn't match. We walked up to the counter at the back of the Coffee Shop.

I didn't turn my head as I walked. I didn't want to stare at anyone. But my eyes darted this way and that. All the kids I saw looked like they were about Julia's age. High school kids—or even older. I felt really young. And *really* short. I tried to act cool, but it's not that easy when you're wearing overalls.

"So, what'll it be?" the guy behind the counter asked. He had long red hair pulled back in a ponytail. He wore a green T-shirt with a steaming cup of coffee printed on the front.

"I'll have a tall iced cappuccino," Jody ordered.

I lowered my voice so I'd sound older. "I'd like a hot chocolate, please."

"Try a coffee, Claud," Jody whispered.

"No, I'll stick to hot chocolate," I said. "Oh, and a donut."

"What kind?" the guy asked.

"What kind of what?" I said.

"What kind of donut?" he asked, leaning forward.

"Oh, right. Well, what kind do you have?"

The guy glanced behind him. "We only have plain left," he informed me.

"Oh. Then I guess I'll take a plain," I said.

As the guy turned around and starting making our drinks, Jody shot me an annoyed look.

"What?" I said.

"Could you have taken any longer?" she muttered.

"It wasn't my fault," I whispered. "If they only have plain, then why did he ask me what kind of donut I wanted?"

Jody shrugged.

The guy behind the counter placed two cups and a donut wrapped in a brown napkin down on the counter. "Will that be all, girls?"

"That's it," Jody said. She handed the guy a ten dollar bill.

When she got her change, Jody stuffed the money back into her pocket and dropped the change into a Styrofoam cup that had TIPS scribbled on it. She sure seemed to know the routine at the Coffee Shop.

"Come on," Jody said. "There's an empty table."

I followed her back across the room and we sat down at a table by the door.

Jody casually sipped her iced cappuccino as she checked out who else was in the room. I put my *very* hot hot chocolate down on the table and sat there, blowing on it to cool it off. I took a bite of my plain doughnut. Not bad.

This really beautiful girl with long brown hair walked by our table.

"Hey," Jody said to her.

"Hey." The girl nodded and smiled back.

"Who's that?" I asked after the girl had gone past.

Jody shrugged. "Just someone I met a couple of days ago."

A guy with a nose ring walked by.

"Hey, girl," he said to Jody. "How's it going?"

"Not bad." Jody smiled.

"Who's *that?*" I asked.

"Just some guy I know." Jody rolled her eyes. "Are you going to ask me about everybody I say hey to?"

"I might," I told her. "What do you do, come here, like, every day? You know *everybody.*"

Jody smiled and took another sip of her cappuccino.

"I don't know one single person," I said, turning to look around at the room. "I mean, who are all these . . . oh, no!" I slid down in my seat. I was doomed. I was caught.

I was in *major* trouble.

"Jody, help!" I whispered.

"What?" Jody asked.

"She's here!" I croaked.

"Who?" Jody said. "Who's here?"

I nodded my head in the direction of the girl at the counter. The girl with long, thick brown hair. The girl with the black leather jacket and black jeans.

The girl who was going to make sure I was grounded for the rest of my life.

"Julia!" I whispered. "Julia's here!"

chapter four

I glanced over at Julia again. She was sitting on a stool at the counter with another girl, talking. Both of them had their heads down, so I couldn't see their faces. But I'd know Julia's hair anyplace.

"Help me, Jody!" I begged. "I have to hide!" I slid down in my chair until I was practically under the table.

"Will you stay chilled, Claudia?" Jody scolded. "Think about it. If it *is* Julia, then she's cutting school, too."

I stared at Jody in astonishment. Julia? Cutting?

I sat up a little straighter. "Maybe," I said. "But maybe she has a free period. The high school kids are allowed to leave campus on their free periods."

"Are you sure it's her?" Jody asked.

"Are you kidding?" I said. "Don't you think I'd know

my own sister? Oh, man—I can't believe this is happening!"

"Claud, sit up more," Jody whispered. "People are starting to look at us."

I glanced at Julia. At that moment, she looked up, too.

I gasped.

"It's not her!" I wriggled back up onto my chair. "I'm saved! Oh, that was a close one, Jody. Her hair is totally identical to Julia's."

"Cool," Jody whispered. "Now will you just mellow out? Here comes Troy!"

Jody smiled and cocked her head slightly to the side.

"Which one is he?" I asked.

Jody whispered back, hardly moving her lips at all, "The outrageously cute one."

Oh, like that really cleared things up for me. There were two guys walking toward us. One had blond hair. The other had brown hair. I didn't think one was outrageously cuter than the other.

"Hey," Jody said, smiling up at the brown-haired guy.

"Hey," the brown-haired guy replied.

Then the blond-haired guy said, "Hey, Jody."

"Hey, Troy," Jody answered.

"Hey," Troy said again, nodding.

I rolled my eyes. Gee, this was really interesting. But I thought I might as well get into the conversation.

I said, "Hey."

"Hey," the brown-haired guy said back. "I'm Scott."

"I'm Claudia," I told him.

"Sit down, guys," Jody offered.

They pulled up chairs from an empty table and sat down. Troy sat backward on his. Right away, he and Jody started whispering to each other. Jody was smiling and giggling. It was as if the two of them were alone at the table.

I looked at Scott and tried to smile. Quick! I told myself. Come up with something to say. Something really interesting.

"So," I said.

"So," he said back.

Okay, it was a start.

Then Scott said, "You like music?"

I felt my tight smile relax into a real one. "I *love* music," I told him. "A lot."

"Me too," Scott said. "I play the sax."

"Yeah?" I said. "Cool. I play the violin. I love the sound of the sax."

Scott smiled. "I think the violin has a great sound, too. I love that Band X song with the electric fiddle."

Now I was out-and-out grinning. "So do I! I think that's why I started listening to them. But now I love all their songs."

"Hey," Troy cut in. "Did you guys hear that Band X is coming to town this weekend?"

"No way!" Jody exclaimed.

"Really," Scott said. "Their concert in Palm Springs got canceled," he told us. "So this morning on KZAK, they announced that they're coming here this weekend!"

"So *that's* why they were playing so many Band X songs on the radio this morning!" I exclaimed.

Scott nodded.

"I can't believe it," I said. "They are, like, my favorite group *ever*. Their song 'Virus'? I could listen to it all day long."

Jody frowned at me. Clearly she thought I'd said something stupid.

But Scott didn't. He said, "Me too. And how about 'Millennium'? Tell me that's not awesome!"

I smiled and zapped Jody a look back.

"Yeah, I like that one, too," I told him.

"Get this," Scott began. "A kid who's a junior at Grant got a block of tickets for the concert, and Troy and I just snagged two tickets in the front section."

"You're kidding!" Jody cried. "That's too cool."

Troy nodded. "It's going to be major. Totally. Everyone's going to be there."

Jody and I looked at each other. Without saying a word we both knew that we had to be there, too. We *had* to get tickets to that concert!

"Hey, maybe somebody at your high school has some tickets, too," Troy suggested.

"Yeah, maybe," Jody said.

Our high school? Grant *was* our high school—or at least it would be when we were old enough.

I stared at Jody. What had she told Troy, anyway? That we were in high school?

"Let us know if you get tickets," Troy was saying. "Then we could meet up at the concert."

"Cool," Jody said, nodding.

"Yeah." Scott smiled at me. "Cool."

I smiled back. The way Scott was looking at me made me feel a little nervous. Did he think Jody and I were, like, fifteen or something? Did he think we'd just made a date? All of a sudden, I needed a little space from this situation.

I pushed back my chair. "I'm going for seconds," I said. "Can I get you guys coffee or, um, anything?"

Troy and Scott shook their heads.

"I'll take another one of these," Jody said, pointing to her empty iced-cappuccino cup.

I stood up—and walked right into Bailey's girlfriend, Sarah!

"Claudia!" Sarah exclaimed. She looked totally confused. "Hi."

"Hi, Sarah," I managed. "Uh . . . how are you?"

I'm doomed, I thought. Sarah will tell Bailey she saw me here, and Bailey will tell Charlie that I cut school! I'm history!

"Claud, what are you doing here?" Sarah asked. "Aren't you supposed to be in school?"

"Um, yeah," I said. "But my English class just got back this big test, and everybody did great on it . . ." I didn't even know what I was saying—I just opened my mouth and started lying.

". . . So the teacher sent my friend and me over here," I went on, "to pick up some donuts for the whole class so we could, like, celebrate."

Sarah was looking at me with her trusting brown eyes and nodding. "Wow, what a cool teacher," she said.

Jody appeared next to me. "I'll get the donuts, Claud," she offered. "How many? Is two dozen cool?"

"Sure," I answered. Jody sounded so sure of herself that all my nervousness disappeared. "Two dozen is cool."

Jody walked off toward the counter and I turned back to Sarah. "So," I said, "what are *you* doing out of school?"

"This a free period for me," Sarah said, smiling. "I'm just picking up some coffee." She held up her paper cup. "Well, I better go. I'm sure I'll see you later."

"See you, Sarah," I said. I waited until she pushed open the door and left. Then I dropped back into my chair.

That was close!

I didn't like lying to Sarah. But it's not like I was lying about anything important, right? I mean, nothing that would do Sarah any harm. She didn't need to know I was cutting. And besides, here I was sitting with two guys who thought that I, Claudia Salinger, was in high school.

I smiled at Scott. He smiled back. "What did you do, cut class?" he asked.

"Yeah," I admitted. "It was boring. I decided to blow it off."

I swear, Scott looked really impressed. "Cool," he said.

"Who was that girl?" Troy asked.

"My brother's girlfriend."

"She's cute," Troy observed.

Jody walked back at that moment with a bag of donuts.

Scott glanced at his watch. "We'd better head out, Troy," he said. Then he turned to me. "Our free period ends in about three minutes."

"See you." Jody gave a little wave.

Troy smiled and squeezed Jody's arm.

Scott smiled and winked at me. Then they left.

"So?" Jody said after the door closed behind them. "What do you think?"

"Cool," I said, nodding. "But what did you tell them, Jody? That we were in high school?"

"Yeah," Jody admitted. "You know that girls' school down the road?"

I nodded.

Jody took two donuts out of the bag. She handed me one.

"Well, you and I are part of St. Joseph's Academy's

freshman class," she said. She licked powdered sugar off her fingers. "And we have a double date with, like, the two cutest guys in the whole tenth grade of Grant High School."

"I can't believe it," I mumbled, my mouth stuffed. "That was really fun. And you know what? Scott plays the saxophone." I giggled. "I can't believe I can pass for fifteen," I told Jody. "Especially in these overalls!"

Jody burst out laughing. "Let's go, Fiddle Girl," she said.

We took the same route back to school as we had going to the Coffee Shop. But this time we didn't run. We walked and munched on donuts.

"I can't believe you actually went and bought donuts," I teased Jody. "What did you think—Sarah was going to count them to make sure we weren't lying?"

Jody threw a half-eaten donut at me.

"I wanted to make it look good," she joked. "Hey! What about that concert this weekend?"

"It sounds really cool," I said. "I wish I could go."

"Well, I'm going home tonight to work on my mom for ticket money," Jody said with loads of confidence. "Band X, here I come!"

"How much do you think tickets are?" I asked.

Jody shrugged.

"I'll talk to Charlie," I said, wishing that I felt as confident as Jody. "When I tell him how much I want to go to the concert, I'm sure he'll give me the money, right?"

"Right," Jody said as we crossed the football field. "I mean, how could he not?"

"He couldn't not," I agreed. "He'll give me the money. For sure."

But even as I heard myself say those words, I realized that I *wasn't* sure.

As we huddled behind a bush near the football field, Jody glanced at her watch. "Fourth period will be over in five minutes," she said.

"It's a good thing we filled up on donuts," I added. " 'Cause we missed lunch."

"Yeah, what a tragedy. No mystery meat or rubber pizza." Jody smiled. "Okay, here's the plan. We'll head straight for the first-floor bathroom," she told me. "Then, when classes break, we'll just go to gym as usual."

"But what if we run into that hall monitor again?" I asked. I was starting to feel nervous. While we were at the Coffee Shop, it was easy to forget about school. But now I couldn't help thinking all my teachers would just look at me and *know* that I had skipped class.

But Jody only shrugged. "So what if we do see the dumb hall monitor?" she said. "So what if she gives us a hard time? Or even turns our names into the principal. It was worth it, wasn't it?"

I grinned at Jody. "For sure," I told her. And this time the words were absolutely true.

We headed for the door we'd come out as if we had

every reason in the world to be exactly where we were. Jody opened the door and peered in.

"It's cool," she said.

We walked in. Kids were in the hallway already, going from the cafeteria to their lockers and the bathroom. We joined them, trying to look normal as we walked into the girls' room.

I washed my hands while Jody put on some lipstick. And when the bell for fifth period rang, we headed out of the bathroom for gym class.

We did it! We cut school!

And we didn't get caught—just like Jody promised. I grinned to myself as I walked down the hallway. Even wearing my overalls, I felt older and wiser than I had that morning.

Who needed school, anyway?

chapter five

I didn't have time to think about the Band X concert during gym class. Or during English, since Mr. Schiller hit us with a pop quiz on *The Catcher in the Rye*. And during seventh period—biology class—I had to pay attention to what Mr. Grodinski was saying about one-celled animals. This test on Friday would be a killer.

But I *couldn't* pay attention. My brain refused. All I could think about was getting to the Band X concert. I tried to listen to Mr. Grodinski. But it was no use. Doesn't matter, I thought. I still have the rest of the week to review bio.

I *had* to go to the concert. I had to! But could I convince Charlie to give me money for a ticket? Money is always pretty tight around our house. What if the tickets were really expensive—like twenty-five dollars or something?

Maybe I could offer to work at the restaurant to *earn* the money.

No, Charlie would think I should help out at the restaurant just because I was a Salinger.

I couldn't think of anything else all afternoon. When school finally ended, I hurried to the school bus. My violin case bumped against my leg as I ran. All I wanted to do was get home and talk to Charlie.

I slid into one of the back seats next to Jody.

"Hey, Fiddle Girl," she said. "Listen, you're sure you'll be able to go to the concert Saturday night. Right?"

"Right!" I exclaimed, feeling more nervous than ever.

But before Jody could say anything else, Caroline Suh walked down the aisle of the bus and sat down in the seat opposite ours.

"Hey, you two," Caroline said. She mostly hangs out with the popular crowd. Today she was wearing this really funky striped cutoff shirt. And her jeans hung really low on her hips. She had a tiny gold hoop going through her pierced belly button.

"Hey," Jody and I said to Caroline at the same time.

"Did you hear who's coming to San Fran this weekend?" Caroline asked.

Before Jody or I could answer, she screamed, "Band X!"

This girl Meg Hubbard, who was sitting in front of us,

turned around in her seat. "Yeah!" she exclaimed. "And I'm going to the concert!"

"Me too!" Caroline squealed. "How did you get tickets?"

"My mom's company is doing the Band X publicity while they're in town," Meg said.

Meg is so lucky. Her mom always gets her tickets to every concert. She acts sort of conceited about it sometimes.

"How did *you* get a ticket?" I asked Caroline.

"My brother bought tickets from somebody at Grant," she told me. "Hey, are you guys going?"

Jody nodded. "We're meeting these two high school guys there."

I couldn't believe it! Did Jody have to tell everybody about Troy and Scott? I mean, it wasn't any of Caroline's business. And it wasn't exactly true—not yet.

"Oooooh, *that* sounds interesting," Meg exclaimed. She glanced at me, running her gaze up and down my overalls. "But you might want to wear something else," she added with a giggle.

"Whatever," I replied. The bus pulled up to the curb at my stop. "See you guys tomorrow."

"Buzz me later, Claud," Jody called after me.

I walked home slowly, thinking. Maybe if I promised Charlie that I'd never ask him for anything else this whole year, he would give me money for a ticket. It was worth a try.

Julia and her friend Justin were in the kitchen when I walked through the door.

"Hi, Claudia," Justin said.

"Hi," I said. "Where's Owen?"

"Watching a video in the living room," Julia told me.

"Guess where we're going this Saturday night?" Justin asked.

I shrugged.

"To see Band X—live!" Julia smiled as she twisted her hair into a knot. "The tour is getting rave reviews."

"I'm going to the concert, too," I announced.

They both stared at me in surprise.

"You got tickets?" Justin asked.

"Well, not yet," I admitted.

"Claudia," Julia said, "you can't go. The tickets are fifty bucks each."

"Fifty bucks!" I exclaimed. Whoa! That was way more than I'd imagined. More than Charlie would give me, that was for sure.

"You don't have that kind of money," Julia went on.

Her know-it-all attitude made me angry. Julia acts like she's so cool just because she's older than me. It's not like she's an adult or anything. I mean, she's only four and a half years older. But she treats me as if I'm a baby.

"For your information," I said with as much confidence as I could possibly fake, "I have my ways."

"What are you going to do, rob a bank?" Julia asked. She and Justin burst out laughing.

"What's so funny?" Charlie asked, walking into the kitchen.

"Oh, Claudia's going to rob a bank," Julia said, giggling.

"Ha, ha," I said. "Very funny."

"Just don't get caught, Claud," Charlie said. "We don't have any money to bail you out of jail."

Things were not exactly going as I'd planned. I sat down on one of the high stools at our kitchen counter.

"Charlie, can I talk to you?" I asked as sweetly as I could.

"Sure, Claud." Charlie pushed his dark hair out of his eyes. He looked exhausted.

Just then Owen burst into the kitchen. "Charlie!" he shrieked. He ran across the room and threw his arms around Charlie's leg.

"Hey, big fella," Charlie said, picking him up and lifting him into the air. "Want something to eat?"

"Eat!" Owen yelled.

Charlie put Owen into his high chair next to me.

"Charlie, can you listen to me for one minute?" I asked him as he took the peanut butter jar out of the cabinet.

"I'm listening," he answered, opening a package of bread.

"I don't know whether you heard or not," I began. "But Band X is coming to town this weekend."

"Mmm-hmm," he said, spreading peanut butter on a piece of bread. Then he cut the bread into four squares and put it on a napkin in front of Owen.

"Juice!" Owen demanded.

"Well, I really want to go to the concert," I went on as Charlie poured apple juice into Owen's cup. "If it's okay with you, of course. And, just so you know, it's like really, *really* important to me to go. So, anyway, I just need some money for a ticket," I finished up.

"She needs fifty dollars, to be exact," Julia put in. She pulled a bag of potato chips out of the cabinet and handed it to Justin.

Charlie looked surprised. "Claud, you know I don't have that kind of money to give you."

"But, Charlie," I said, "I could pay you back."

"Are you kidding me?" Charlie asked. "Where would you get money to pay me back? I'd have to advance you your allowance for weeks, and then you'd end up with no spending money. No way, Claud."

I sighed, glancing over at Julia and Justin. They sure were no help. They just sat there, munching on chips and watching me plead with Charlie. It looked as if they were enjoying the whole scene.

"Even if I could spare fifty dollars," Charlie added,

"which I can't, you're too young to go to a concert by yourself."

Uh-oh. I hadn't even thought about this. What if Charlie wouldn't even *let* me go to the concert?

"I wouldn't be going by myself, Charlie," I told him. "Jody's going, too. We'll go together."

"You think *that* would make me change my mind?" Charlie exclaimed as he wiped up some juice Owen had spilled on the counter. "Jody isn't exactly chaperon material."

I groaned. Why couldn't Charlie understand how important this was to me?

"But this might be the only chance I'll have in my whole life to see Band X!" I argued. "Plus Band X has this really amazing violinist, Jam, and hearing her live might be totally inspiring for me. As a musician, I mean."

Charlie kept wiping the counter. He didn't even glance up at me. Did he have a heart of stone?

"Okay, think about this," I went on. "Band X might not come back to San Francisco for years! By the time they have another concert here, I might be, like, twenty or something—and it would be too late!"

Julia made a snorting sound when I said that, and then she burst out laughing. "Claud!" she exclaimed. "You are too much!"

I whirled around to face her. "What do you care?" I

46

yelled. "You already have your ticket. You don't have to ask permission. So go ahead—laugh!" I turned back to Charlie. "If no one in this family cares enough to lend me the money for a ticket, then I'll just have to find another way to get one!"

"Claudia, please!" Charlie snapped. "Stop acting like such a baby. And speaking of babies . . . Julia, check out Owen's T-shirt. It's disgusting!" Charlie began wiping peanut butter off of Owen's hands. "Why is he wearing such a dirty shirt?"

"Don't look at me," Julia told him.

Oh, great! I thought. Charlie and Julia have totally forgotten about my Band X ticket. Now they're back to talking about the stupid *laundry* again!

"It's not my turn to do the wash this week," Julia continued. "It's Bailey's!"

"You called?" Bailey said, walking into the kitchen. He had a big smile on his face.

"Yeah," Julia told him. "I was just telling Charlie how it's *your* turn to do the laundry."

"Julia! You know you owed me a turn for the time I did the wash for you last month," Bailey replied.

I sighed. Then I got up, took a cereal box out of the cabinet, and climbed back up on my stool. As I munched Frosted Flakes straight from the box, I watched my brother and sister argue. I could have been watching a tennis match. Back and forth, back and forth. As I watched and munched, I kept trying to figure out how I was going to get to the Band X concert.

Finally Bailey shook his head. "Forget it, Julia," he said. "I'm not going to let you ruin my good mood."

"Why are you in such a good mood, Bay?" I asked.

"Because I have the greatest girlfriend in the world," he answered.

"Uh, you do?" I squeaked.

Oh, no! I thought. I totally forgot about Sarah! She had seen me in the Coffee Shop this morning! She knew I wasn't in school!

I put the cereal box on the counter and waited for Bailey to say how Sarah had told him about bumping into me. I waited for the conversation to turn from laundry to cutting school.

"This weekend is our anniversary," Bailey continued.

Hey! This didn't sound like the start of a cutting-school conversation.

"And Sarah is taking me to see Band X," Bailey went on. "They're giving a concert in town this weekend."

"Yeah, Justin and I are going, too," Julia told Bailey.

"Maybe we should all go together," Justin added. "Where are your seats?"

Everyone was going to the concert—everyone but me! This was definitely not fair.

While they tried to figure out where they were sitting, my brain was hard at work. Bailey was in a great mood. I mean, who wouldn't be, going to the concert and all? And since Sarah had bought the tickets, maybe Bailey had some cash he'd be willing to lend to an adorable younger sister.

"Hey, Bay?" I said. "Jody and I want to go to the Band X concert, too. How about lending me fifty dollars for a ticket?"

I glanced over at Charlie. He gave me a tired smile and rolled his eyes.

"Aw, Claud. I wish I could," Bailey said. "But I don't have any money."

"You don't?" I asked.

He shook his head. "I just spent my last dollar on this really amazing anniversary present for Sarah."

"Oh. That's cool," I said. But I wasn't ready to give up. Not yet. "Well, listen. If I manage to get a ticket," I went on, "would you and Sarah take Jody and me to the concert? I *swear,* you wouldn't even know we were there."

"Any other time, I would, Claud. But it's our anniversary," Bailey said. "Sarah and I don't exactly want company. And besides, we have, like, the whole evening planned."

"Well, I hope you two have a great time," I said. I tried to make my voice sound as sad as possible. But nobody seemed to notice.

I slid off the stool, grabbed my backpack and violin case,

and stomped upstairs to my room. I tossed my stuff down and threw myself onto my bed. Then I reached over and turned on the radio.

"... *Hear one of the all-time hot Band X tunes, 'Virus'!*" the voice of Danny Rose announced. And the song came on. I turned up the volume, closed my eyes, and let the music take me away from my problems. But when I heard Jam's electric fiddle at the end of the song, I felt tears stinging my eyes.

I can't believe everybody gets to see them except me, I thought. It's just not fair!

"*That was Band X, and this is KZAK. Have I got some dynamite news for all you guys out there who are looking under rocks, but still can't find a ticket to the big Band X concert. Listen up, guys and gals, 'cause . . .*"

I sat straight up on my bed. I was all ears.

"*. . . Station KZAK knows how you all love Band X—and that's why we're giving away free tickets!*"

chapter six

"Free tickets!" I shouted.

"Yes, rock-and-rollers! Your favorite station for all the hits, KZAK, will be giving away forty tickets a day—two tickets at a time—from nine to five for the next three days! Get your pens and pencils ready! Danny Rose is going to feed you all the details!"

I grabbed my backpack and scrambled around for a pen and paper. Oh, why had I given Pete Hennesey that pen, anyway? I mean, sure he was cute and all. But he wasn't worth two free tickets to see Band X!

My fingers felt something smooth and plastic on the bottom of my pack. I grabbed it and pulled it out. A pen! Danny Rose was already talking, so I didn't have time to find a scrap of paper. I wrote down the details on the palm of my hand.

"*. . . For the next three days, every time we play a Band X song, the first listener to call 555–KZAK and correctly identify the song and tell what CD it's from will win a free pair of tickets!*"

I grinned as I wrote the phone number on my hand. I knew every Band X song by its first two notes! And I knew which CD every song was on, too. I was sure to win!

Band X, here I come!

I pulled the phone from the hallway into my room. I punched in Jody's number.

"Jody?" I cried when she picked up. "You're not going to believe this!"

"What?" she said.

"We are definitely going to see Band X!"

"Charlie's giving you money for a ticket?" Jody gasped. "Cool! My mom's not even home yet, so I haven't asked her."

"It doesn't matter," I told her. "Charlie wouldn't give me the money. But we're going to *win* two free tickets!"

"No way," Jody said. "How can we do that?"

"KZAK is having a contest," I said. "For the next *three days*, every time they play a Band X song, the first person to call up and name the song and tell which CD it's on, wins two, I repeat, *two,* tickets to the concert!"

"Claudia!" Jody exclaimed. "We're there!"

"We're there!" I practically screamed. "Yes!"

"Hey, wait a second," Jody cut in. "Is the contest on all day long?"

"I think so," I answered. "He said something about nine to five."

"Claudia—hello? We can't listen to the radio in class," Jody pointed out.

Oh, no! She was right! I felt as if someone had just punched me in the stomach.

There has to be some way, I thought. I have to get those tickets. "Well . . . maybe I can listen to my Walkman during lunch and . . ."

"And what?" Jody said. "Run to a pay phone, wait in line, and hope we're the first callers?"

"What was I thinking?" I said miserably. "We're never going to get to that concert!"

"Oh, yes we are." Jody's voice was full of confidence.

"But how?" I asked her. "How can we listen to the radio and call in from school?"

"We can't," Jody declared. "That's why we're not going to go to school."

"What?" I cried. "You want to skip school for three days? Are you crazy?"

"Chill, Claud," Jody told me. "Do you want to go to the concert as much as I do?"

"So much! You totally can't imagine."

"You want to meet Troy and Scott, the sax player, as much as I do?"

She *had* to throw in the saxophone part. "Absolutely," I answered.

"Then all we have to do is cut school tomorrow," she told me. "We'll sit by the radio with your phone—and when they play a Band X song . . ."

"Bingo!" I cut in. "Two concert tickets will be ours!"

"Right," Jody said. She sounded happy. But I didn't really feel any better.

"Jody?" I said. "Cutting a couple of classes wasn't hard. But how are we going to cut a whole day? I mean, we'll definitely get caught."

"It's easy," she told me. "Here's the plan. Get dressed tomorrow morning as if you're going to school. Leave your house at the usual time and wait for me at the end of your block. That way your family will think you went to school."

"Okay."

"Then we'll go back to your house and hang there for the day."

"Hold it," I said. "Charlie doesn't take Owen to day care until nine. What about *your* house?"

"No good," she said. "My mom's in and out all day. But I've got it. We'll meet at the Coffee Shop. We can hang there until nine and then go to your house."

"That should work," I agreed.

"And, oh, *don't* take the school bus across town in the morning," Jody added. "Take the trolley or something."

"Why?" I asked.

" 'Cause you don't want anyone to see you."

Wow, Jody really thought of everything. She has a way of making things sound so easy.

I was nervous. Okay, really nervous. But when I thought about Band X tickets, I knew I could do it—no problem.

Well, maybe *one* problem.

"Wait! I forgot about my biology test," I told Jody. "I was totally spaced out during the review today. I couldn't concentrate at all. I'll get an F if I'm not there the rest of the week."

"Claud, you've never gotten an F in your life," Jody said.

"But science is hard!" I argued. "I mean, it's an advanced biology class. I really need the review."

"Okay, what if I listen to the radio and call in when they play a Band X song?" Jody suggested. "That way you'll be able to get in lots of quiet study time. More than if you were at school."

"But if *you're* going to listen, why do *I* need to skip school?" I asked.

"Because you know more about Band X than I do," Jody replied. "You'll always know which song it is, and which CD it's on."

"I guess you're right," I said.

"So, Fiddle Girl, what do you say?" Jody asked.

"Well . . ."

I heard laughter from downstairs. My brother and sister, laughing because they were happy about going to the Band X concert. They totally didn't care about me being stuck at home without a ticket.

That did it.

"Definitely," I told Jody. "Let's do it."

Wednesday morning, I woke up before my alarm went off. I lay in bed, staring at the ceiling. Yesterday, I'd cut class for the first time. And today I was going to cut a whole day of school. Charlie would ground me for sure if I got caught.

But the whole thing is his fault, I thought. I mean, if he gave me the money to buy a ticket, I wouldn't have to cut school!

I crawled out of bed and pulled open my closet door.

Whoa! It was a good thing I wasn't going to school, because I had nothing—truly nothing—to wear. Absolutely everything I owned was in the laundry. I scrounged around on a top shelf and found a pair of black leggings.

I had seen a button-down denim shirt hanging over the banister of the stairs last night. It was probably Bailey's. I stuck my head out of my door and looked for the shirt. It was still there! I snatched it up and quickly put it on.

If Bailey didn't want me wearing his clothes, he could do the laundry like he was supposed to.

I rolled up the sleeves as I walked down to the kitchen. Owen was sitting in his high chair making a mess with a banana and some Cheerios.

"Morning, Owen," I said, kissing him on the head.

"Cla-dee!" Owen yelled, showing his mouthful of banana.

Julia sat at the counter, spooning yogurt out of a container and flipping through a magazine. She was still in her bathrobe.

A horrible thought struck me.

"Julia!" I exclaimed. "Are you sick? Are you staying home from school today?"

She glanced up at me. "Thanks for your concern," she said, giving me a curious look. "But I have a free first period today. I'm just taking it easy this morning."

Relief flooded through me. "Oh, well, I'm glad you aren't sick."

Charlie sat at the table reading the paper, as usual. But there was nothing "usual" about his clothes—a rumpled, too-small pink shirt with a button-down collar and corduroy pants.

"Charlie?" I said. "Where did you get that shirt?"

He sighed. "It was lying under a suitcase on the floor of my closet," he told me. "I bought this thing for a date when I was in high school. It's pretty old."

I giggled. "That's really old," I agreed. *"Ancient."*

I stuck a Pop-Tart into the microwave. I wasn't really hungry. In fact, I felt too nervous to eat. But I thought I should do everything I usually did in the morning. I didn't want my brothers and sisters to get suspicious.

Bailey walked into the kitchen next. He had on jeans and a plaid shirt I didn't remember seeing before.

Charlie glanced at him. "Slept over on the couch again, huh?"

Bailey nodded and yawned.

"Nice shirt, Bay," I said.

He frowned as he poured himself a bowl of cereal. "Sarah lent it to me when I told her how desperate I was."

"That's *Sarah's* shirt?" I asked.

Julia laughed.

"It's her cousin's," Bailey told me, shooting a look at Julia. "Her *boy* cousin's. He left it at her house."

"This is ridiculous!" Charlie exclaimed. "We're all down to no clothes. As head of the household, I order you, Bailey, and you, Julia, to do the laundry *together* tonight."

"But I have a chem quiz—" Bailey began.

Charlie cut him off. "No buts."

"I won't be home tonight," Julia informed him. "I have to go to the library until really late."

The microwave went off, and I grabbed my Pop-Tart. "Bye, everybody!" I interrupted their argument. "See you tonight!"

I left the kitchen. I'm acting normal, I told myself. Nobody noticed a thing. Nobody would even guess that I'm going to cut school.

I headed for the door. Oops! I almost forgot to take my backpack. I ran up to my room and grabbed my pack. For a second, I stared at my violin case. I always took it with me. But today, I decided to leave it behind. My brothers and sister never came into my room. No one would notice that I hadn't taken it to school.

I ran down the stairs of my house to the sidewalk. I walked to the corner—as usual. Then, with a quick glance over my shoulder, I turned left instead of right. I walked two more blocks and caught the trolley. Fifteen minutes later, I walked calmly into the Coffee Shop.

I spotted Jody right away. She was sitting at a table by the window.

"Hey," I called to her as I walked up to the counter and got in line. The same redheaded guy was working there as the day before.

"What'll it be?" he asked when my turn came.

I opened my mouth to tell him hot chocolate, but what I said was, "I'll have a double iced mochaccino, please."

Then, with my iced mochaccino in hand, I joined Jody at her table. I felt older with my coffee—and really cool.

"Hey, Claud," she greeted me. Then she lowered her voice and added, "Guess who's here and walking our way."

I froze. "Sarah?" I whispered, thinking that I couldn't explain what I was doing here two days in a row. I couldn't lie to Sarah again!

Jody didn't answer. I don't think she even heard me.

"Hey, Jody. Hey, Cheryl," Troy said.

I was so glad he wasn't Sarah that I didn't even feel too insulted that he didn't remember my name. But of course I corrected him.

"That's Claudia," I told him. "I'm Claudia."

"Hi, Claudia," Scott said, coming up behind Troy.

"Hi, Scott," I answered. "So do you guys, like, live here or something?"

"I could ask you the same thing." Scott laughed.

"Yeah, I guess you could." I laughed, too.

"Nah," Troy put in. "Scott and I just like a little caffeine in the morning."

Then he smiled and reached out for Jody's hand.

I took a sip of my iced mochaccino. "We have to stay wide awake today, too," I said, flashing a glance at Jody.

She got my meaning—we had to be totally alert to be the first callers to KZAK!

"Hey, did I tell you guys?" Jody said. "We got tickets to see Band X! Right, Claud?"

I couldn't answer. I was too busy choking on my mochaccino! Why was she telling them we already had tickets? I knew we *would* win a pair. But still. I didn't see why she was lying about it, saying we already had tickets.

"Very cool," Troy was saying. "Hey, why don't we all meet in front of the stadium fifteen minutes before the concert starts?"

"That's a great idea, Troy," Jody told him.

"Yeah. Great," I choked out.

"Great," Scott added. "Come on, Troy. Algebra calls."

"See you, Jody," Troy said. "Bye, Carla."

"Claudia," I called after him. "It's *Claudia.*"

"He is, like, way too cute," Jody said, watching Troy walk out the door.

"Jody!" I exclaimed. "Why did you tell them we'd meet them before the concert? We don't have tickets yet."

"But we *will,* Claud," Jody said. "By the end of the day we will each have a ticket to the concert. Trust me."

chapter seven

So, you think it's safe to head over to your place?" Jody asked me.

I glanced at my watch. It was a quarter to nine.

"Charlie and Owen should be leaving in about ten minutes," I told her. "Yeah, I guess we can start heading over there now."

Jody and I left the Coffee Shop and walked to the trolley stop. We didn't have much of a wait, which was a good thing. I didn't want anyone asking us why we weren't in school. We jumped on the trolley.

"I hardly slept last night, thinking about the concert," Jody said, yawning. She dropped onto a wooden bench. "I'm sort of tired."

"I was tired, too," I said. "But now I feel totally wide awake. My heart is racing."

Jody started to laugh. "Congratulations!"

"Congratulations?" I asked. "For what?"

"You, my friend, are experiencing your first caffeine rush. That's what you get for drinking coffee instead of hot chocolate."

"Wow, you really think that's what it is?" I asked. "The coffee?"

"Absolutely."

I grinned. I usually drank hot chocolate. But not today. I usually went to school. But not today. Who knew what other wild, new things today would bring?

"Hey, this is our stop," I said.

We grabbed our stuff and jumped off the trolley. We started walking toward my house.

"We have to make sure Charlie is gone," I said as we turned my corner. "He's, like, permanently late."

Jody nodded. "Let's cut through the backyards," she suggested. "That way we can see if his truck is in the driveway before he can see us."

Jody and I climbed a hill in someone's front yard and went around back. Then we moved quietly through yard after yard, squeezing through hedges at the property lines. At last we came to the yard next to mine. We peeked through the bushes.

"His truck's not there," Jody whispered.

She pushed a branch aside and began crawling under the bush.

"Wait!" I called in a hoarse whisper. "I forgot—Julia!"

"What about her?" Jody asked.

"She's got first period free today," I told Jody. "She might still be home."

Jody ducked back under the bush. "Well, how do we find out?" she whispered.

I shrugged. We stared at the house in silence for a minute.

"What time is it?" Jody asked.

I checked my watch. "Nine-twenty."

"If Julia's second period class starts at nine-thirty," Jody whispered, "then she'll be gone."

I nodded. "Right. Let's go."

We made our way across the backyard. It felt weird to be sneaking up to my house this way—like I was breaking in or something.

I put my key in the lock and jiggled it until it caught. Then I pushed the door open and we tiptoed inside.

The house was quiet.

Then I heard something. A high-pitched squealing noise.

"What's that?" I whispered as we walked into the kitchen.

"Just the furnace or something," Jody said. "Don't worry. Where's the radio? We have to get started!"

"Right," I agreed. "Charlie has a boom box. Wait here. I'll get it." I ran up to Charlie's room. I didn't see the radio right away, but then I found it under a damp towel. I grabbed it and started back to the kitchen.

But as I reached the stairs, I stopped. There was that high-pitched noise again. And this time I recognized it.

It was music.

And it was coming from Julia's room.

My heart began beating so fast, I could hardly breathe.

Slowly I edged toward the stairs to Julia's attic bedroom. Was my sister still home? Did she have *second* period free, too?

Or was *she* cutting school?

I climbed the stairs and listened outside her door. I could hear someone singing.

"Claudia!"

I jumped.

"Claudia! What's taking you so long?"

It was Jody, downstairs.

I couldn't exactly yell down to her to be quiet!

Quickly, I gave Julia's door a little tap. It creaked open. I stuck my head inside. I checked the bed. The desk. The closet. No Julia.

Julia's clock radio was playing. She must have forgotten to turn it off when she left! I let out a big sigh of relief.

I ran downstairs. Jody was waiting for me in the front hallway.

"What did you do, stop to make the beds?" she asked.

"I thought I heard Julia," I explained as I led the way into the living room. I plugged Charlie's radio into an outlet and set it on the coffee table. I turned it on.

Jody and I listened for a second.

It was the Beatles.

"This isn't KZAK," Jody said. She squatted in front of the radio and fiddled with the tuner.

Seconds later we heard strains of a dance song.

"Got it," Jody said. She turned the volume up full blast. Then she plopped down on the couch.

I sat down next to her. But my heart was still racing a little from the coffee. Or maybe from my close call in Julia's room. I couldn't sit still.

"This is boring," I said. I jumped up and started dancing around the living room. When a song by the Compactors came on, I grabbed Owen's plastic hammer and pretended it was a microphone. I jumped up on the coffee table and lip-synched with the lyrics:

"Girl, you've got to break out of that cage! Girl, you've got to step up onstage!"

"Come on, Jody!" I yelled over the music. "Dance!"

"Man, Claudia." Jody shook her head. "You've got too much energy in the morning."

"Come on!" I jumped off the coffee table and grabbed Jody's hand. I yanked her up off the couch.

"Follow me!" I commanded. I started doing the Electric Slide.

Jody sighed. "You're so lame," she commented. Then she smiled. She waited a couple of beats and joined in. Together and totally in step, we danced all around the living room until the song ended. Then we both flopped down on the couch, giggling.

Suddenly the first notes of "Brainiac" blasted out of the radio. This was it! A Band X song!

Jody and I looked at each other. Then we both leapt off the couch.

"The phone!" I screamed. "Where is it?"

"Didn't you get it?" Jody cried.

"I thought *you* got it!"

"No!" Jody shrieked.

"Ahhhh!" I ran for the kitchen. I scanned the countertop, but I didn't see the cordless phone. I moved all the newspapers off the table. No phone. I pulled open the refrigerator. No phone.

"Did you find it?" Jody yelled.

"Not yet!" I yelled back.

Where was that stupid phone?

I glanced at the floor under Owen's high chair—and there it was.

"Got it!" I shouted. I scooped up the cordless phone. Frantically, I started punching in numbers.

555–KZAK, I told myself. *555–KZAK.*

I held my breath and waited for an answer. All I got was a big fat busy signal.

"Rats!" I exclaimed. I ran back to the living room. "It was busy."

"Maybe you dialed wrong," Jody suggested, grabbing for the phone. She punched in the numbers. We both put our ear to the phone.

"Busy." Jody made a face and hung up.

"I don't get it," I complained. "How could it be busy? I mean, a radio station should have call waiting or a receptionist or something!"

"I don't know," Jody said. "We were too slow that time. But next time all we have to do is just hit redial."

She set the phone on the coffee table, right next to the radio. We sat down on the couch and stared at the phone.

"Okay. The next Band X song they play, we are ready," I said. "They'll play another one soon."

"Yeah," Jody agreed. "So we missed one song. Big deal. Danny Rose said he's giving away forty pairs of tickets each day, right? So all we have to do is wait here and be ready."

"Right."

"Right."

We stared at the phone some more.

Danny Rose played lots of songs, both old and new.

Jody and I resisted dancing and lip-synching. We wanted to be ready for the next Band X song.

And suddenly, there it was—one of my favorites, too. I leaped for the phone. But so did Jody. Our heads banged together and the phone slid off the coffee table and onto the floor.

"Ouch!" Jody yelled. She fell back on the couch and began rubbing her head.

I lunged for the phone and hit redial. "Busy!" I cried, dropping the phone onto the rug. "I can't believe it!"

Jody groaned. "Oh, well," she sighed. "That's only two down. Say we missed two songs before we got here this morning—we still have sixteen chances to go."

"Right," I agreed. "No problem. I mean, it's not like *everyone* is staying home from school to listen."

We stayed glued to the radio all morning. Every time Danny Rose played a Band X song, we hit redial and got . . . busy, busy, busy.

When "News at Noon" came on, I figured it was safe to take a break. Jody was asleep on the couch. I nudged her awake.

"Lunch?" I asked.

"Mmmph," she said. She rubbed her eyes.

I went into the kitchen and grabbed two bowls and four boxes of cereal. I managed to carry it all back into the living room.

Jody looked impressed. "Why thank you, my good waitress," she said, faking an English accent. "I always come back to Salinger's restaurant because of its talented waiters."

"Oh, we are so glad," I tried to say with my idea of an English accent—which isn't half as good as Jody's. "We do aim to please our customers."

"By the way," Jody added, "your manager, Charlie Salinger, is such a handsome lad. Do you happen to know if he is involved with anyone in particular?"

Jody has the biggest crush on Charlie. It's really annoying.

"I don't believe he is, at the moment," I replied. "But, my dear, do you know that he is quite cheap? Yes, so cheap that he wouldn't even lend his little sister money for a very important concert."

"Well, I never!" Jody exclaimed. "What a rat!"

"*Big* rat," I agreed.

We combined the different kinds of cereal in our bowls. "Milk?" I asked.

Jody shook her head and began eating with her fingers. "It's better dry."

I was reaching for my cereal when the phone rang. My heart stopped beating. Who was calling during a school day? What was I supposed to do?

Jody and I stared at each other as it rang a second time. "Who do you think it is?" I whispered.

Jody shrugged. "Are you going to answer it?"

I shook my head. "I'm not supposed to be here."

The phone rang a third time and the answering machine picked up. We listened as Charlie's voice said:

"Hi, you've reached the Salingers. Please leave a message after the beep and someone will call you back. Thanks a lot."

BEEP!

"Hello, this is Mrs. Lipman at the Walt Whitman Junior High attendance office," said the voice on the machine.

I grabbed Jody's arm. My heart began beating wildly.

"We ask that a parent or guardian call us back to tell us the reason for Claudia Salinger's absence from school today," Mrs. Lipman went on. "The number is 555–5900. Thank you."

She hung up and a loud dial tone filled the room.

I gasped. "Jody!" I cried. "It was the school! They know I'm cutting!"

chapter eight

Chill, Claud," Jody said calmly. "They don't know you're cutting. If nobody calls in to say you're out sick or something, Mrs. Lipman always calls your house. It's no big deal. Don't worry."

I groaned. "But what if they call Charlie at the restaurant?"

"They won't!" Jody declared. "You never miss school. You get great grades. You are a *perfect* student. They don't go after students like you."

"Are you sure?" I asked, starting to feel a bit better.

Jody nodded. "They only go after students who are always out—like me."

"You think they called your house?" I asked.

Jody shrugged. "Probably," she said. "I'll erase the message before my mom hears it."

"Good idea," I said. I pressed the rewind button on the answering machine.

"But," Jody went on. "Even if my mom hears it, she won't do anything about it. It's like she's given up even *trying* to punish me." Jody shook her head. "Who cares? It's better than some stupid lecture about school being important."

"I don't know," I said softly. "I'd give anything in the world to have my mom give me a great big lecture." I thought about Mom. What would she think about me cutting school? She wouldn't be too happy about it, that was for sure. I promised myself to practice my violin an extra half hour to make up for what I was doing.

"Aw, Claud," Jody said. "I'm sorry. I didn't mean—"

"It's okay," I told her. "But Mrs. Lipman said that a parent or guardian was supposed to call her."

"No biggie," Jody said. "You just get an answering machine at the attendance office when you call. I do it all the time, and I say I'm my mom."

Amazing. Jody knows, like, *everything* about skipping school. I put my hands on my hips. "Yeah, but how do I make my voice sound like Charlie's?"

"So say you're Julia," Jody suggested. "Mrs. Lipman is not going to check your records to see who your legal guardian is, believe me."

"Julia, huh?" I asked. Then I held out the phone to Jody. "Here, you do it."

"No problem," Jody said, taking the phone.

My heart was racing as she dialed 555–5900, listened for a few seconds, and started talking.

"Hello, Mrs. Lipman," Jody said. "This is Julia Salinger, Claudia Salinger's elder sister calling."

Elder? I put my hands over my mouth to muffle my giggles. But I had to hand it to Jody—she sounded a lot like Julia.

". . . An upset stomach," Jody was saying into the phone. "She should be back in school tomorrow. Thank you."

She hung up and took a little bow.

"You're good," I admitted. "Very good."

Jody plopped down on the couch. "I'm still hungry," she said. "Don't you have any pretzels or anything?"

"There weren't any in the cabinet," I said. "But we might have more stashed in the basement—we use it as a pantry."

I walked to the door that led to the basement stairway. Jody followed. When I opened the door, we both jumped back.

"Phew!" Jody cried. "What's that smell?"

I sniffed the air. "I don't know. It smells like mildew or something."

"Go check it out."

"Come with me."

"Are you afraid to go down into the basement by yourself, Fiddle Girl?" Jody asked.

"I am when it smells like something died," I said. "Just shut up and come with me."

Jody followed me down the basement steps. It was really dark until I pulled the chain that turns the light on. I almost turned the light back off when I saw the mounds of laundry heaped on the floor around the washer and dryer.

"Maybe these clothes have started to stink," I said. "They've been sitting here for weeks."

"I don't think clothes can smell like that," Jody said doubtfully.

"Well, I'm going to do what you said and wash some of my things," I said.

I walked over to the washer. I lifted the lid and peered in.

The mildew smell almost knocked me over.

"Yuck, nasty!" I cried, jumping back. "Gross!"

"What *is* that?" Jody pinched her nose with her fingers.

"Somebody left a load of wet clothes in here," I told her, looking in again. "They must have been in here for a week or something, because they're really moldy and disgusting!"

"Eeeeew. Let's get out of here before I hurl," Jody said.

"I can't just leave this stuff in here to get even stinkier," I told Jody. "You're the big expert on doing laundry. Help me figure out how to work this machine."

Jody made a face, but she walked over to the machine.

"Here," she said, turning a dial on top to FULL CYCLE. "Where's your detergent?"

I handed her the jug, and she dumped in a capful. Then she pulled out the dial and the machine started running.

"You may have to wash this stuff a couple of times to get the smell out," she advised. "But, hey—this is a start."

"Thanks, Jody," I said. "It smells better already."

We climbed the stairs back up to the living room.

"I'm sick of staying in here," she said, pulling out the radio plug. "Let's go up to Julia's room."

"I don't know," I said. But Jody was already on her way upstairs. I picked up the phone and followed her.

Jody wandered into Julia's room. She plugged in the radio. I stood in the doorway and watched as she opened Julia's closet.

"Pretty empty in here," she commented.

Jody took a scarf out of Julia's closet and threw it around her neck. Then she stood in front of the mirror and clipped her hair up in the front—exactly the way Julia does.

"Um, hi," Jody said, mimicking Julia's voice. "My name is Julia, and I think I'm super cool."

I started giggling.

In a few minutes, Jody had on one of Julia's best dresses—one she'd worn to a prom. She sat down at Julia's dressing table and put on some of her dark brown lipstick.

"Oh, baby!" she exclaimed, checking herself in the mirror. "Wouldn't Troy love to kiss these luscious lips?"

"Really," I told her.

Jody brushed on some mascara. Then some blush. Then she paraded around the room, giving me a fashion show.

"Excellent!" I applauded. "Totally Julia!"

Jody took off that dress and put on another one.

"Don't forget about the barrette," I reminded her.

For the next half hour, Jody imitated Julia—her voice, her walk, her attitude, and, of course, her wardrobe. When she finished, I gave her a big round of applause.

Twice, while Jody was changing into a new outfit, I ran down to the basement and put more loads of clothes into the washer. I figured out how to start the dryer on my own.

Three times while we were in Julia's room, KZAK played a Band X song. Each time, I was right there, hitting the redial button on the phone. But I never got anything but the same old busy signal.

"Maybe school is, like, totally empty today," I said to Jody. "Maybe everybody stayed home to win free tickets."

"Maybe," Jody said, as she unzipped a slinky black dress of Julia's. It fell to the floor and she stepped out of it.

"Hey, what time is it?" she asked.

I checked the clock on Julia's night table.

"Oh, wow! It's three-thirty. School is almost over!"

"I got to get out of here!" Jody exclaimed. "Let's meet at the Coffee Shop again tomorrow morning."

"What?" I cried. "No way! We can't cut school two days in a row!"

"But we have to!" Jody exclaimed. "Or we can't go to the concert!"

"Yeah, but . . ." I began.

"Claud, what's one more day?" Jody asked. "Come on! Please! We had such an amazing time today, didn't we?"

She had a point. "I guess."

"I know we'll be lucky tomorrow," Jody finished up.

I sighed. "I sort of forgot about all that studying I was going to do today for my biology test," I said.

"So you can study tomorrow. You'll get so much done," Jody said. "I swear, I'll handle the radio and the phone. All you have to do is study."

"Oh, okay," I said at last. "But you have to *make* me study. Even if you have to sit on me to make me do it!"

Jody grinned. "Cool," she said. "See you at the Coffee Shop."

I walked Jody downstairs and watched as she skipped down our front steps. Then I checked my watch again. Whoa—it was almost four! Julia would be home with Owen in less than five minutes!

I zoomed into the living room. It was a total pigsty. I grabbed the cereal boxes and bowls and ran them into the kitchen. I practically threw them into the sink. Then I grabbed the Dustbuster, ran back into the living room, and sucked up all the cereal and crumbs that covered the floor. I straightened up the couch cushions and wiped off the coffee table.

Whew! I plopped down on the couch to catch my breath. A key clicked in the front door. Julia.

Julia! Oh, no! Julia was home! And I'd forgotten all about her room! It was a disaster!

chapter nine

I bolted up the two flights of stairs to Julia's attic bedroom.

I scooped up the black dress that was wadded up on the floor and hung it up in record time. I did the same with the prom dress that Jody had tossed on the bed. Next, I grabbed scarves from the floor and tossed them onto the shelf of Julia's closet. Finally, I stuck all the tops back onto Julia's lipsticks. I only hoped they were the right tops! Finally, I grabbed Charlie's radio.

I jumped when I heard Julia's voice.

"Claudia? What are you doing in my room?" Julia demanded. She stood in the doorway, holding Owen on her hip.

"Hi, Cla-dee!" Owen waved.

"Hi, Owen," I said sweetly. "Did you have a good day at school?"

"Claudia," Julia repeated. "I asked you what you're doing in *my* room."

"Nothing. Uh—borrowing a barrette." I picked up the barrette Jody had thrown on the bed.

"Borrowing *my* barrette without *my* permission in *my* room is not nothing," Julia said, snatching the barrette out of my hand.

"Well, you borrowed my brush yesterday," I said. *"And* two months ago you borrowed my—"

"Claud, whatever," Julia interrupted. She looked as if she were getting a major headache. "Just get out of here."

"I'm gone," I said. "Come on, Owen." I took him out of Julia's arms. "Let's go play cave people in my old tent."

As I climbed downstairs with Owen, I thought about my first day of cutting school.

It was a blast!

Thursday morning, I met Jody at the Coffee Shop again. This time when the guy behind the counter asked me what it would be, I ordered a *decaf* mochaccino. I'd had enough close calls the day before to make my heart beat like crazy. I didn't need caffeine.

I sat down at the table with Jody. She was sipping an iced coffee, looking around the room. "I don't think Troy's here," she muttered.

"Bummer," I said. But I must have sounded like I didn't mean it, because Jody shot me a nasty look.

We left the Coffee Shop just after nine, taking the trolley back to my house. We didn't cut through any backyards, though, because Charlie had left early with Owen to run some errands.

We walked into my empty house through the front door.

Jody plopped down on the couch in the living room and I ran upstairs to get the radio.

"Let's listen in the kitchen today, okay?" I said when I came back downstairs.

"Why?" Jody asked me. "I'm comfortable here."

"Yesterday you took off and left me with all the cleanup," I told her. "The place was a sty! I had like five seconds to clean everything up before Julia walked through the door."

With a sigh, Jody heaved herself up off the couch and followed me into the kitchen. I plugged in the radio and put the phone right next to it. Then we sat on high stools at the counter and listened. I knew I should leave the listening to Jody and start cramming for my bio exam, but I didn't think I could find the energy for studying.

Jody spun around on her stool. "Ah," she sighed. "This is the life."

"I guess," I said. "Hey, listen! That's a Band X song!"

Jody grabbed the phone and dialed KZAK. "Busy," she said.

"Figures," I added.

Jody pressed the OFF button on the phone. "So," she began, "aren't you psyched about our double date Saturday?"

"We don't have a double date."

"Hello? Of course we do! We're meeting up with Troy and Scott before the concert."

"And then what?" I asked her. "We sit in the parking lot while they go in and listen to the music?"

"No, dummy," Jody wrinkled her nose. "We'll probably all sit together. Or maybe Scott and you will sit in his seats, and Troy and I will sit in our seats."

"Our seats?" I practically shouted. "We don't *have* any seats! We can't even get a living breathing human being on the phone at KZAK!"

"Relax," Jody advised. "We'll get tickets. Don't worry." She whirled around on her stool again. "Maybe Troy will hold my hand during the concert," Jody murmured.

"Maybe," I said, not that I cared at all.

"So, what are you going to wear for Scott?" she asked.

"What do you mean 'for Scott'?"

"Guys like when you wear special outfits for them."

"Oh, puh-*lease!*" I said. "Like I care what a guy wants me to wear. But that reminds me. I think I'll stick another couple of loads in the washer today. That way if, by some miracle, we *do* get tickets, at least I'll have clothes."

I hopped off my stool. "Stick close to the phone," I told her. "I'll be right back."

I ran down to the basement. While I was throwing clothes into the washer, I thought about what Jody had said. I felt sort of annoyed with her today. I was starting to think that Troy was the only reason Jody wanted to go to the concert. He's all she talked about—holding Troy's hand, what outfit she'll wear for Troy. Every time I brought up Band X's music, it was like she wasn't interested.

I got the laundry going and ran back up to the kitchen. Jody had made us toast and jam. I had just taken my first big bite when it happened.

The phone rang.

Without a word, Jody and I jumped up and ran into the living room. We waited for Charlie's message to end and for the answering machine to pick up. Then we heard a voice say:

"Hello. This is Claudia's math teacher, Ms. Holtz."

Oh, no! Why was my teacher calling? I shot Jody a terrified look.

"Claudia, I'm just calling to let you know that I've decided to give your class a test on Monday. I didn't want you to miss out on studying. But if you're still out sick

84

tomorrow, we'll arrange for you to take it later next week. I hope you're feeling better soon."

I sank down on the couch as the message ended and the machine started going through its beeps and clicks.

"I feel awful," I told Jody.

"What, you're sick?" she asked.

I shook my head. "No," I said. "I feel bad that people at school think I'm really sick. And that Ms. Holtz is nice enough to call me about the test." I shook my head. "I feel like I've let everybody down."

Jody groaned. "Get over it, Claud. You haven't!"

I shrugged. "I might as well have," I said. "Plus now I have a math test to study for—"

"It's next week!" Jody broke in. "It's *after* the concert!"

I let out a long breath. This whole staying home thing was getting complicated. Now I was missing the review for *two* tests. And if we didn't get Band X tickets, it would all be for nothing.

"Okay, Jody, back to the phones!" I ordered. "We are going to get a pair of tickets between now and three-thirty—or else!"

Jody grinned. "I like your attitude."

The rest of the day we sat with the radio directly in front of us. Every time Danny Rose played a Band X song, I pounced on the phone.

The third song, I screamed, "Jody! It's ringing!"

Then someone picked up.

"Hello!" Danny Rose's deep voice said on the phone.

"Hello," I screamed into the phone. "Hello, Danny!"

"You've reached KZAK—home of alternative music . . ." Danny's voice went on.

I started getting a bad feeling in my stomach as I listened.

". . . and sponsors of the Band X cross-country tour! I'm sorry. You are not one of the first ten callers for this song. But keep on rockin' and keep your radio tuned to KZAK!"

"What? What?" Jody was yelling at me as I listened.

I slammed the phone down on the counter. "I got a recording!" I shouted. "I can't believe it!"

"A recording?" Jody looked as if she couldn't believe it either.

"Do you think some people have super-speed dialers on their phones or something, Jody?" I asked. "I mean, I can't believe we've been beat out on every song!"

"Me either." Jody sighed. "Well, I guess a recording is one step closer to tickets than a busy signal."

"I guess," I agreed. But for the rest of that afternoon all we got was busy, busy, busy.

By three-fifteen, I was wiped out from doing nothing all day, except for eating too much and listening to the radio too hard. Worst of all, I hadn't even cracked open my biology book.

"Well, at least we tried," I told Jody as she got ready to leave. "See you on the bus tomorrow morning."

"The bus? What do you mean?" Jody exclaimed. "We can't go to school tomorrow! It's the last day of the contest. We can't give up now!"

"But . . ." I began. "I mean, we said we'd skip school one day, and it's already been two days—"

"I can count," Jody snapped.

"Well, I give up," I told her. "We're never going to win those tickets. And besides, I can't miss another day of school! I have my biology test tomorrow! I must have been out of my mind to cut school today."

"Listen, Claud," Jody said softly. "We can't give up now. I just know we'll get lucky tomorrow!"

I shook my head no.

"Listen, I bet a lot of people are giving up right now," Jody said. "So, that makes it better odds for us. There will be fewer people listening tomorrow. I just know we'll get through."

"I can't!" I pleaded. "I'm already in so much trouble—"

"But listen to my plan, okay?" Jody interrupted.

This was the first I knew that Jody had a plan. I nodded.

"I'll go to the first three classes of the day tomorrow, while you stay here and study and listen to the radio. And then . . ."

"And then what?"

"And then I'll cut out of school during fourth period

and come over here and take over. *I'll* listen to the radio while *you* go to the last classes of the day. This way, you won't miss your science test." She grinned at me. "It's perfect, right?"

"I don't know," I said again. I didn't love this plan. But tomorrow really was our last chance for concert tickets. And it did seem silly to give up after spending two whole days trying to get into the contest. Plus, this way I could study in the morning and take my science test in the afternoon.

"Okay," I said at last. "We'll go with your plan."

"You're the best!" Jody exclaimed, giving me a high five. Then she grabbed her backpack and headed for the door.

"Wait a second," I said, grabbing her arm. "Promise me, Jody. Promise me that you won't be late getting here tomorrow."

"I, Jody Lynch, promise you, Claudia Fiddle-Girl Worrywart Salinger, that I will *not* be late." Jody grinned at me.

I grinned back at my best friend. I couldn't help it. Tomorrow would work out fine. Right?

chapter ten

*B*rrrng!

"That's the doorbell!" I called from my room. Ever since dinner, I'd been holed up there, madly cramming for my bio exam. "Can someone get it?"

Brrrng! Brrrng!

"Hey, down there!" I yelled. "Someone's at the door!"

"I'll get it!" Bailey shouted.

Even though I didn't want to be disturbed to answer the door, I *did* want to know who it was. I walked over to my bedroom door and peeked out.

"These are notes for Claudia," I heard a girl's voice say.

I froze. Who was that?

". . . For when she was out," the girl went on.

"Out?" I heard Bailey say.

I sprang from my room, tripped over Owen's blocks, and stumbled downstairs. There stood Sari. She was holding a bunch of photocopied biology notes. I practically tore them out of her hand.

"Hey, Claudia," Sari said. "How are you feeling?"

"Oh, you know, surviving," I said. "Thanks. Listen, I don't want you to get whatever I've got. See you!" I slammed the door in Sari's face.

Bailey stared at me. "Claud, I'm confused."

"That figures, Bay. You're always confused." I tried not to sound nervous.

"Claudia, did you cut Mr. Grodinski's class?"

What should I do? I couldn't just *lie* to him, could I?

"Oh yeah, like, right, Bay," I babbled. "I cut class right before my big biology test." I shook my head. "No, what happened was, I had to go to the nurse in the middle of class." I rolled my eyes. "Can't a girl have some privacy in this house?"

"What I'd like to know is, can't a girl have some clean clothes in this house?" Julia asked as she walked down the stairs. "I'm down to my prom dresses, Bay."

"Yeah, well, lucky you," Bailey said. "I'm down to nothing! Nothing at my apartment and nothing here!"

"Bailey, you are totally trying to snake me into doing the laundry for you again," Julia shouted. "And I won't!"

For once, I was thrilled to hear them argue. I edged my way past them and took Sari's notes back up to my room. I shut the door behind me and leaned against it. I felt like I might faint. That was *way* too close.

I was lucky Bailey bought my story. And that Julia interrupted before he could ask me any more questions.

It's not worth it, I thought. I am never cutting school again.

Except tomorrow.

On Friday morning, I walked out our front door, went around the block, and cut through a neighbor's yard to our backyard. I hid there until Charlie's truck pulled out of the driveway. Owen looked so cute, sitting in his car seat. I could tell he was all excited about going to "school."

As I made my way across our backyard, I wished I were going to school, too. The KZAK contest and cutting school had gotten totally out of control. Sure, I really wanted to go to the concert. And yeah, it would be fun hanging there with Jody and Troy and Scott.

But I felt awful about lying to everyone. And about slamming the door on Sari. *And* about the bio test I was sure to fail. I was totally lost, even with Sari's notes.

I let myself into the house and ran upstairs to get the radio. Then I grabbed a box of cereal and the phone and went into the living room. I turned the radio on. I opened my biology book and started cramming for my exam, which was only five hours away.

Whenever Danny Rose played a Band X song, I dialed as

fast as I could. But I only got his stupid recording once. The other four times, it was the busy signal.

Every time I turned back to my bio book, all the little one-celled plants and animals seemed to swim in front of my eyes. I couldn't remember which was which. After an hour, I slammed my notebook shut.

I'm doomed, I thought. I'm going to fail this test no matter what I do.

So I picked up Charlie's radio and the phone and headed for the basement. I might as well do something useful with my morning.

By the time Jody knocked on the back door, I had finished pairing the last of the Salinger socks. Everything we owned was clean. I don't know what Bailey and Julia keep complaining about. Laundry isn't *that* hard.

"Any luck?" Jody asked as I let her in.

I shook my head.

"Well, go to school and ace your test," she said as she sat down at the kitchen counter.

"Yeah, right." I rolled my eyes.

"Because," Jody continued, "by the end of the day we will be the proud owners of two tickets to the Band X concert!"

I picked up my backpack from the counter. Then I stopped.

"Uh-oh," I said. "We forgot. I need a note for the

attendance office to get back into school. Will you write one for me, Jody? I mean—Charlie?" I said, smiling.

"But of course!" Jody grinned.

I watched as Jody took a pen and pencil and forged my note.

> *To Whom It May Concern:*
> *Please excuse Claudia Salinger's absence. She missed school because she was sick.*
> *Thank you,*
> *Charles Salinger*

Jody handed me the note. I checked it over. No spelling errors. I stuffed it into my pocket.

"Don't make a mess," I warned Jody. Then I headed off to school.

When I got there, lunch was just ending. I dropped the note off at the attendance office. Then I headed for gym. If I'd thought about this plan a little longer, I would have gone back to school *after* gym. I'm the worst basketball player in history.

As I walked down the hall, I saw my first-period teacher, Mr. Chandler. Uh-oh! Would he remember that I wasn't in social studies this morning?

Okay, act normal, I told myself. I grabbed my bio notes from my backpack and pretended to be studying them as I walked past Mr. Chandler. Don't look at him, I ordered myself. Just don't look up.

I looked up.

Mr. Chandler was staring at me with a frown on his face.

I quickly glanced back down at my notes. He couldn't really remember every student who showed up to class. Right?

Wrong.

"Claudia?" Mr. Chandler called.

I stopped walking and looked up at him. "Uh, hi, Mr. Chandler," I said, trying to sound normal.

"I'm surprised to see you here, Claudia," he told me. "You weren't in my class this morning."

"Um, yeah, I know." I began talking really fast. "Well, I sort of . . . had to watch my little brother this morning. I just got to school ten minutes ago."

Mr. Chandler didn't say anything. He just kept looking at me.

"I have to get to gym," I said. "But I'll definitely see you in class on Monday!" I didn't wait for him to say good-bye. I just ran toward the gym.

I made it through gym and English. Then came biology. Sari gave me a curious look as I took my seat. I knew I owed her an apology for slamming the door on her—but it would have to wait until after the test.

I barely survived the exam. It was tough. Really tough!

There were two essay questions on it that I had to leave blank. I've never done that before. Usually I know enough to come up with *something* to write.

At last biology ended. As I walked down the hallway to Spanish, I thought the worst was over.

I was wrong.

Someone tapped me on the shoulder. I turned and found myself face to face with Mrs. Fremont, my guidance counselor.

"Hi, Claudia. I saw from Mrs. Lipman's absence sheet that you've been out sick for a couple of days," Mrs. Fremont said. "Are you feeling better?"

"Um, yeah. Thanks," I managed. I felt my heart pounding against my rib cage. This was turning into the worst day of my entire life.

"Mrs. Lipman also mentioned that your brother Charlie hadn't returned any of her calls," she went on.

"Calls?" I said. My brain was spinning. How many times had Mrs. Lipman called? I'd only heard one message from her on our machine. Were there others that I missed? Had Charlie heard them?

I noticed that Mrs. Fremont was still waiting for an answer.

"Oh! Well, you know, Charlie's pretty busy at the restaurant, Mrs. Fremont," I said quickly. "He figured since I was better now, he really didn't have to call."

I swear, I had no control over what was coming out of

my mouth. I could hardly even hear myself over my pulse pounding in my ears. What if Charlie heard Mrs. Lipman's messages? What if he found out I was cutting?

"Claudia," Mrs. Fremont said at last. "Your teachers tell me you also missed some of your classes this morning, and some on Tuesday morning. I think it would be a good idea if Charlie came in to meet with me next week."

"Next week?" I shook my head. "Next week is totally booked for him. He's doing, like, ten wedding receptions at Salinger's next week, and he's totally busy."

Maybe *ten* was a few too many, but I wanted to impress her with the fact that no matter what, Charlie couldn't come in!

Mrs. Fremont just kept staring at me. Out of the corner of my eye, I saw kids standing near us in the hallway, watching and whispering. I had to end this . . . and fast!

"You know Charlie supports me and my brothers and my sister," I kept babbling, "so he can't really afford to take off from work."

"I'm aware of your home situation, Claudia," Mrs. Fremont said gently. "And I admire Charlie's dedication to your family. However," she added, "if you miss any more school, I will insist on a meeting with Charlie. Are we clear on this, Claudia?"

"Very," I said, trying for a smile.

"And Claudia?" Mrs. Fremont added as I turned away

from her. "If you ever need anyone to talk to, remember, I'm here for you."

"Uh, thank you."

I practically ran down the hallway to Spanish class. I felt totally guilty. How could I just lie to my guidance counselor like that? How could I pretend Charlie was too busy to even call the attendance office?

Because, I answered myself, I couldn't tell her the truth:

"Oh, thanks, Mrs. Fremont. I wasn't really sick. Actually, my best friend and I were hanging out at my place phoning in to KZAK to win tickets to the Band X concert. Don't worry. After the concert, I plan to attend school on a regular basis."

I reached my seat in Spanish class and dropped my head down onto the desk. What if Mrs. Fremont called Charlie to insist on a meeting?

She won't, I told myself. She won't call him unless I miss any more school.

And I'm never missing school again. I'm never lying to a teacher, or a guidance counselor, or my family ever again.

My cutting days are over.

chapter eleven

As the school bus crept toward my stop that afternoon, I wondered how our house looked after Hurricane Jody had swept through it. I crossed my fingers and hoped that Jody didn't make a mess. And that she had won us two tickets.

And that nobody else got home before I did.

When I reached the house, I ran up the front steps and pushed open the front door. The entryway hadn't been trashed. So far, so good. I walked inside and went into the living room. There was Jody, stretched out on the couch, reading a magazine. The radio was on the coffee table, but it wasn't turned on.

"Jody? What happened?" I asked.

Jody sat up and smiled. "Which do you want first?" she asked. "The good news or the not-so-good news?"

"The good news, please!" I told her. "After today, I need some good news."

"Okay," Jody said. "Here it is—we're going to the concert tomorrow night!"

My mouth fell open. Then I started yelling and jumping up and down. "All right!" I shouted. "You did it! You are the greatest, Jody Lynch!"

I plopped down on the couch beside Jody and let the good news sink in. It was worth it—all the cutting school and lying was totally worth it. I was going to see Band X!

"So you finally got through to KZAK," I said. "What song did you identify?"

"Well, no song," Jody told me.

"Huh?"

"We didn't win the radio contest," Jody confessed.

I stared at her for a couple of seconds. A bad feeling in my stomach was starting up.

"Wait." I shook my head. "I don't get it. You just told me that we're going to the concert."

"We are."

"Jody . . ."

"Calm down. The contest ended at three. I never even got through. I was so bummed. And then Danny Rose made this big announcement. He said Band X was putting more tickets on sale and there's this special deal at Record World at the mall—"

I didn't let her finish. "So, you're telling me that I cut

school for nothing?" I yelled. "That I flunked my bio test for nothing?" My voice was shaking now. "That the last three days have been for *nothing?*" I felt like crying.

"Claud, you're not listening to me. They put more tickets on sale and—"

"Oh, that's great," I cut in again. "On our way to Record World, I'll just *steal* the money for the tickets."

"Will you let me finish?" Jody shouted. "Record World is putting five hundred more tickets on sale, but—" She paused dramatically. *"But*—the first hundred people in line get tickets for *free!"*

I let that sink in for a minute. Free. Free tickets. "Are you saying what I think you're saying?" I asked.

"Yup." Jody grinned. "All we have to do is be two of the first hundred people in line and we're there!"

We high-fived.

Jody settled back on the couch. "Of course," she added, "we *will* have to spend the night in line."

"What?" I cried.

"Well, other people will be trying to win the tickets," Jody pointed out. "We'll have to get there super-early to be in the first hundred."

"Are you crazy, Jody?" I demanded. "Have you gone bonkers?"

"What's the problem?" Jody asked. "I thought you'd be psyched about this."

"I'll tell you the problem," I said. "Charlie. He'd never *ever* let me spend the night at the mall, standing in some line."

"Hello, Claud?" Jody was grinning again. "That's no problem. Because you're not going to tell Charlie. He'll never know and he'll never find out."

"Why not?" I asked her.

"Because you'll say you're spending the night at my house," Jody explained. "And I'll tell my mom I'm staying here." She held her palms up. "What could go wrong?"

"I don't know." I shrugged. "You think it's safe?"

"Totally. Everybody does it. When hot concert tickets go on sale, everybody sleeps outside the place that's selling them. It's a way cool thing to do. It's like a big pre-party for the concert. And it's not like we'll be alone. There will be hundreds of fans doing the same thing."

"I don't know, Jody. It seems sort of scary," I admitted.

"It won't be," Jody promised. "You'll see."

"Still," I said. "I don't want to lie to Charlie anymore."

"Claudia, we deserve these tickets," Jody declared. "We've worked so hard to get them. Please! Don't give up now!"

I thought about it. "Maybe you're right," I said at last. "I mean, nobody in my family even tried to help me get a ticket. And I did everybody's laundry, which no one even noticed. I *do* deserve to go to this concert. And Charlie will never find out I slept at the mall."

"No one will find out," Jody agreed. "And after this, you won't have to lie to Charlie anymore, and you won't have to skip school."

"Okay," I finally said. "But we have to leave *now*. Julia will be home with Owen any second, and I don't want her asking me a million questions about where I'm going."

Jody waited while I stuffed a sweater and my tooth-brush into my backpack. Then I pulled my sleeping bag down from the shelf of my closet. Jody helped me carry my gear as we walked the fifteen blocks to her house. On the way, we talked over our plans.

"You can call Charlie at the restaurant and tell him that you're sleeping over at my house," Jody said.

I hoped that wasn't going to be a problem. Charlie wasn't wild about me hanging out with Jody. He usually puts up a fight when I say I want to spend the night at her house.

"And then I'll leave a note for my mom saying I'm at *your* house," Jody continued. "Mom won't be home until after we're gone—she has a date tonight."

Jody unlocked her front door and we walked into her house.

Jody's mom is hardly ever there when Jody gets home—she has to work late a lot. And when Mrs. Lynch *is* home, Jody is usually fighting with her. I mean, Jody loves her mom and all, but they don't always get along too well.

We went into Jody's room. She showed me different outfits that she was thinking about wearing to the concert.

"Wear this," I said, picking up a white T-shirt with cool stitching around the collar. "It's great."

"Nah," Jody said. "But *you* can borrow it for the concert."

"Really?"

"Yeah. I bet Scott will like it."

"Jody! Forget Scott," I said, blushing. "But, well, okay. I'd love to borrow it. Thanks!" I folded the T-shirt neatly and put it in my backpack.

Next, I picked up Jody's phone and called Charlie at the restaurant. Time for my absolutely last-ever lie to Charlie.

"Hi, Charlie!" I said, trying to sound casual.

"Hi, Claud. What's going on?"

"I'm calling from Jody's house," I told him. "Can I sleep over here tonight?"

"Uh, what?" Charlie said.

I heard dishes crashing in the background.

"I asked if I could stay at Jody's house tonight."

"No."

"No? Why not?"

"For one thing, we have dinner at the restaurant tonight. You know—family dinner?"

Ouch! I couldn't believe I'd forgotten about family dinner. All five of us have dinner together at least once a week—*every* week. We've been doing that ever since Mom and Dad died. I *never* forget about it. Especially because I'm the one who usually makes sure that we do it.

And I'd forgotten all about it. I glanced at Jody. She was packing her stuff in a bag for tonight.

What am I supposed to do? I thought. How can I miss family dinner?

"Claudia?" Charlie said.

Jody motioned for me to hurry up. I sighed. I had spent too much time trying to get these tickets to back out now. I promised myself that this would be the one and only family dinner I'd miss. *Ever.*

"Charlie, please?" I whispered into the phone. "Jody really needs me here with her tonight. She had a huge fight with her mom, and I'm trying to help her work things out. Please! It's important."

Jody put her hands over her mouth. She was cracking up.

On the other end of the phone, Charlie let out this really big sigh. "I don't know, Claud," he said.

"Please, Charlie," I begged. "It's not a school night. I'll be home by eleven tomorrow morning."

"Okay, okay," Charlie said. "If that's what you really want to do, go ahead." He paused for a moment, and then added, "We'll miss you at dinner tonight."

I hung up the phone and gave Jody a thumbs-up. But I didn't really feel happy. I'd never missed family dinner night before. The thought of not being there made me feel awful.

"Okay, let's go," I said.

"One sec," Jody said. She pulled out a piece of looseleaf paper and scribbled a note to her mom.

Mom—there were no messages. I'm crashing at Claudia's tonight. See you tomorrow. Jody.

Before leaving, we raided the kitchen for munchies. We stuffed pretzels, popcorn, crackers, cheese, Pop-Tarts, potato chips, and bottles of water into our packs.

Then we picked up our sleeping bags and set off for Record World.

"Tonight is going to be awesome," Jody said.

I nodded. But all I could think of was my family, spending tonight without me.

chapter twelve

W e're doomed!" I cried. "There are like a million people here!"

I wasn't kidding. There were tons of people already standing or sitting in the mall outside Record World. I tried to count them as we quickly walked to the end of the line.

"I got ninety-two people," I told Jody as we staked out our place behind three boys wearing tie-dyed T-shirts.

"Good," Jody said. "That means we're number ninety-three and ninety-four. That puts us in the first hundred!"

"But, Jody," I said, "what if I counted wrong? Or what if some of these people are saving places for their friends?"

Jody frowned. "I don't think they can do that," she said. But she didn't sound too sure.

More and more people came and lined up behind us. Everyone looked older than us. Some people were carrying coolers and huge picnic baskets. Before long, there must have been, like, a hundred people behind us. Jody was right. We weren't going to be alone in the mall.

For the first couple of hours, Jody and I had a blast. All the mall stores were open and there were lots of people walking by. We sat against the wall and people-watched. Jody made up a game where we took turns pretending that every seventh guy that walked by was our future husband. Whenever a "future husband" passed by, we cracked up.

After a while, we got sick of playing that. I fished some paper and pens out of my backpack and we played hangman. By the time we got sick of that, the mall was pretty empty. All the stores had closed up. The lights were out, and big metal gates had been rolled down over the display windows. Cleaning crews came by with wide brooms and funny-smelling cleaning products. The people on line grew quieter. Lots of people fell asleep.

I glanced around. I had never been in the mall after hours before. The whole place didn't seem real—I felt as if I were in a dream or in a movie or something.

"I sure hope we're in the first hundred," I told Jody. "What if we're like a hundred one and a hundred two or something?"

"Stop it, Claud!" Jody shook her head. "I'm sure we're in the first hundred. We have to be, right?"

I shrugged. Neither of us said anything for a while. Then Jody took a walk, to see where the line ended.

"You won't believe it!" she said when she came back. "There must be a thousand people in this line."

"I thought they were only selling five hundred more tickets," I said.

Jody shrugged. "Maybe some people do this for fun."

I grinned. "Yeah, it *is* kind of fun."

Lots of people in line had portable radios. They all tuned them in to KZAK, which was playing nonstop Band X songs. It was like a mini rock concert!

Jody and I spread our sleeping bags out and had our picnic on top of them. We shared our popcorn with the guys in front of us in line. They gave us some of their M&Ms. We found out they went to high school in the south part of the city, and they knew an amazing amount of stuff about Band X.

They had been to three other Band X concerts before, and they described all three. I was having a blast. I mean, the concert would be great. But being in the line was a way cool event all by itself.

So cool I almost forgot about missing family dinner.

I checked my watch after we finished eating. It was almost midnight. We still had a long night to get through. I felt tired. But I didn't like the idea of actually going to sleep on the hard, cold floor of the mall—even though the guys in front of us were already snoring.

It was getting chilly. I pulled my sleeping bag up around my legs like a blanket.

"Don't tell Scott and Troy how we got the tickets," Jody said. "Okay?"

"Why not? It's a pretty good story."

Jody shrugged. "But it's not cool."

"I thought you said this *was* cool," I said, confused. "I thought you said everybody did it, and it was really cool."

Jody only shrugged again. "Just don't say anything, okay? I mean, I know what I said. And it *is* cool, hanging out here with you, Claud. It's just not cool for Troy and Scott to know exactly how we got our tickets. Know what I mean?"

"I guess."

But I didn't. Not really. Sometimes Jody acts like guys are totally different from girls. Whenever she's around a guy that she likes, Jody sort of stops acting like herself. I don't get it.

I was too tired to think about it much.

A little after two o'clock in the morning, Jody sat up and peered toward the front of the line. "Hey, look!" she said. "A guy's handing out the bracelets!"

"Bracelets?" I said. "They're giving us free bracelets?"

Jody rolled her eyes. "They have numbers on them," she explained. "So Record World will know where you were in line. And people who come late can't cut in front of you."

"I get it," I said. "But Jody! Now we'll find out for sure if we're in the first hundred."

Jody and I watched this skinny blond guy wearing a Record World T-shirt walk along the line, handing out bracelets. They were made of bright red plastic.

I wrinkled my nose. "They look like hospital bracelets," I whispered.

Jody didn't say anything.

The blond guy walked closer and closer to us. With every step, he had fewer and fewer bracelets in his hand.

At last he reached us. He was only holding three red bracelets.

"Here you go," he said, and he handed Jody number ninety-eight and me ninety-nine.

"Wow!" I exclaimed as I slid my arm inside the bracelet and pressed down the metal clip. "Talk about close calls!"

Jody put her bracelet on, too. We both looked at the numbers for a minute. Then we threw our arms around each other and jumped up and down, screaming and laughing.

We were going to the Band X concert!

Numbers one through ninety-seven were celebrating the same way. Then after a while, we all calmed down and it got quiet again. Everybody turned off their radios. It was really dark.

Jody and I sat there in our sleeping bags, waiting. I

stared at my watch. The time seemed to crawl slowly by. It reminded me of watching the clock on Tuesday morning—the first day I cut classes. Boy, I thought, that morning seemed like years ago. Now I was practically a pro at cutting school!

As it got later, I felt more and more uncomfortable sitting on the floor. Even with my sleeping bag, the tiles were really hard. Plus, they must have turned the heat off or something, because now it was freezing! I eased down into my sleeping bag, wishing I'd brought a pillow.

"What did they do, forget we were in here?" I asked Jody. "It's so cold!"

"Yeah, I know," she murmured. "What time is it?"

I pulled my arm out of my sleeping bag. "Um—it's a little after four," I said, yawning.

Jody groaned. "Six more hours of this!" She fell back onto her sleeping bag.

I was sort of hungry, although my stomach felt funny. Probably from all the junk food I had eaten instead of dinner. And I was getting colder by the minute. I always get cold when I'm tired. I don't know why. Charlie told me that Mom was the same way. But I don't remember that about her.

Thinking about Mom made me miss her. I wished I had brought my violin case with her picture in it, so I could take it out now and see her.

My mind wandered to the family dinner at Salinger's—the dinner I missed. I was incredibly happy to have a Band X ticket. But was it worth missing dinner with my family?

Not really, I thought drowsily. Not to me. If I had it to do over again, I would definitely go to the dinner.

I pictured Charlie sitting at our favorite booth in Salinger's—and jumping up dozens of times to check on things at the restaurant. I pictured Bailey, talking about Sarah, with that really happy look he gets in his eyes. I imagined Julia, brushing her hair out of her face and wiping dinner off Owen's face. And I thought about little Owen. I could almost hear his baby voice saying, "Where Cla-dee is?"

At that moment, I missed everybody in my family so much, I felt like crying.

I didn't want to cry. I was already cold and hungry and tired. I didn't need red, itchy eyes, too. I sat up in my sleeping bag and poked Jody. But she was sound asleep.

So I just sat there, staring. I watched this tall guy with very short blond hair and a goatee walk up and down the line. He looked like a high-school guy. He had gigantic arm muscles.

After a while, I noticed that he kept stepping on people's feet. He always said he was sorry and acted like it was an accident. But he did it over and over again. Some people told him to cut it out. But most people ignored him.

Then he stopped pretending it was an accident. He just

kept walking up and down the line, kicking at people who were asleep.

What a jerk, I thought. I glanced at my watch. A quarter to five.

I looked up again—and saw the blond guy. He was staring at me!

He began walking toward us with a mean look in his eyes.

All of a sudden, I felt wide awake.

Wide awake and *scared!*

chapter thirteen

The guy came closer and closer to us. I hunkered down in my sleeping bag. I tried to look invisible. My heart was beating like a drum. I was so scared!

The guy shuffled by us. Suddenly he kicked Jody's feet.

"Hey!" Jody yelled. She sat straight up in her sleeping bag. "Cut that out!"

The guy grinned. "What are you going to do about it, little girl?" he asked loudly. "Call your mommy?"

"Leave us alone," Jody snapped.

My heart was racing now. Why did Jody have to talk to him? Why couldn't she ignore him like everybody else was doing?

"Aren't you too young to be out here alone in the

middle of the night?" The guy leaned over us, giving us a nasty smile.

"Get out of here!" Jody yelled.

His smile faded. He leaned even closer. "If you know what's good for you," he began, "you'll give me your bracelet and run along home to mommy."

"You run along home, jerk," Jody told him.

The guy sneered at her. "What are you going to do?" he asked. "Make me?"

I sat frozen in my sleeping bag. This was a nightmare. A total nightmare.

What do I do? I thought frantically. What am I supposed to do?

"Beat it," Jody told him. "Or I'm calling the cops."

Good idea, I thought. This was getting out of hand. Somebody should call the cops. So what if Jody and I get into trouble for being here without permission? At least we'll be alive!

"Yeah?" the guy was saying. "And what will the cops do when they find two little girls out at night all alone? I bet you're runaways."

"Oh, give it a rest," Jody told the guy. "Get lost!"

"Hey, dude!" some guy farther back in the line shouted. "Leave those girls alone!"

"Get out of here, man!" someone else yelled.

I felt a tiny bit better. All these other people were here. *Older* people. They would make him go away.

But all of a sudden, the guy lunged forward. He grabbed me by the wrist.

"Stop it!" I screamed. "Let go of me!"

But he didn't let go. He grabbed my bracelet and tried to pull it off my arm. I screamed again.

The three boys in front of us sprang up and pulled the guy away from me. Two of them dragged him toward the doorway of the mall. A woman behind us yelled that if he came back, she was calling the police.

The blond guy didn't even glance at me as they dragged him away.

"Are you okay?" the third guy in front of us asked.

"Sure," Jody said bravely. "We're fine." But her voice was shaking.

Me, I was shaking all over. I couldn't stop.

The guy knelt down in front of me. "Don't worry," he said. "I'll look out for you girls. Everything will be cool."

"Thank you," I whispered.

Tears rolled down my face. I wanted to go home. I wanted Charlie or Bailey or Julia. Sleeping here had been a bad idea. A very bad idea.

"Jody, I want to go home," I whispered, trying to choke back my tears.

"Claud, it's okay," Jody said. "The guy's gone. He won't bother us again."

"I don't care," I told her. "I'm scared. I don't feel good. I really want to go home."

116

"But how can we get home now?" Jody asked. "Think about it, Claud. We can't exactly walk around the streets at this time of night. Even taking a taxi would be pretty scary. And if we leave this line, we might run into that creep outside the mall."

She was right. We couldn't leave in the middle of the night. I could call Charlie, I thought. He would come rescue us.

But then he would ground me forever. He would never forgive me for lying about sleeping at Jody's house. He would probably never even let me hang out with her again.

I took a deep breath and checked my watch. It was almost five-thirty. In another half hour, the sun would be up! This awful night would be over.

I sighed. "I guess I'll make it," I told Jody.

"Why don't you try to get some sleep?" Jody suggested. "I'll stay up and make sure everything is all right. I promise."

I nodded and wiggled down into my sleeping bag. I closed my eyes and pretended to play my violin inside my head. That always calms me down.

I guess I did fall asleep, because the next thing I remember was Jody shaking me to get up. I felt so tired. And so stiff from sleeping on the floor. I yawned and stood up.

"The line's moving," Jody told me.

We quickly stuffed everything back into our packs and rolled up our sleeping bags.

Little by little we got closer to Record World. At around ten-thirty, numbers ninety-eight and ninety-nine stepped up and showed the woman behind the window two red bracelets.

"Here you go, girls," the woman said, handing us each a red ticket. She smiled and added, "Now go home and take a nap so you won't fall asleep tonight at the concert!"

We stepped away from the ticket window and gazed at our tickets. I couldn't believe it. We did it. We really got tickets!

Jody hugged me. "We rule, Fiddle Girl," she said. "We're going to the concert!"

We said good-bye to the guys in front of us. "See you tonight!" Jody told them with a smile. Then we headed out of the mall.

Jody stopped right outside the exit. "Here, give me your ticket, Claud," she said. "I'll stick both these babies in my pack where they won't get lost." She slid the tickets into a compartment inside her backpack. Then she zipped it up. "Boy, I can't wait to meet Troy and Scott tonight. Can you? It's going to be amazing!"

All the way home, Jody chattered about the concert— what she was going to wear, what she was going to say to Troy. I only half listened. I was so tired I could hardly see. I didn't care about Troy and Scott at all.

"See you," I said when we reached my corner. "Thanks for not letting me give up!"

Jody grinned. "Call me around six tonight, okay?" she said. "I know I'm going to crash—but I don't want to sleep through the concert!"

"I'll call you," I promised. Then I turned and began walking up the block to my house. All I could think about was taking a hot shower and crawling into bed. Every bone in my body ached.

I was about three houses away from home when I noticed a car parked in front of our house.

I wonder who that is? I thought.

I walked closer and saw that it was a white car. A white car with a blue stripe.

I froze. Parked in front of our house was a *police* car!

chapter fourteen

The police! At my house!

I started running. Something awful had happened! Someone must be hurt!

I dashed up the front steps and shoved open the door. I ran inside. "Hey!" I cried. "Where is everybody?" I dropped my backpack and my sleeping bag and ran back to the kitchen.

Charlie and Julia sat at the table. Bailey sat on a stool at the counter. Beside him stood two police officers. They were all staring at me. But—where was Owen?

"Where's Owen?" I cried. "Is he okay? What happened to him?"

Charlie let out a huge sigh. "Claud, you're all right," he said.

"What about Owen?" I screamed.

"He's in the living room, watching a video," Julia told me.

"Nothing happened to Owen," Bailey said. He walked over and put his arms around me. "But we thought something had happened to you." He hugged me tightly. I felt his cheek against mine, and it was damp.

What's going on? I thought. Was Bailey crying?

Why was he crying if everybody was okay? Why were the police there?

Suddenly I understood. Why everyone looked so worried. Why the police were there. They were there because of *me!*

I put a hand to my mouth. I looked from Charlie to Bailey to Julia again. They all had red, bloodshot eyes. They looked as if they had been up all night.

The police officers picked up their hats from the counter. One of them came over to me. "Are you all right, Miss Salinger?" he asked.

I nodded. "Yeah," I whispered. "I'm fine."

"I'm glad you're home safe and sound," the police officer said.

"Me too." I told him.

"It doesn't always turn out that way," he went on, shaking his head. "You caused your family plenty of worry last night."

I nodded.

"I hope staying out all night won't become a habit," his partner added.

"No," I whispered. "It won't."

Charlie stood up. "Thank you," he said to the police officers. "We appreciate your help. I can handle it from here."

Bailey walked the police to the front door and let them out. The instant the door closed, Charlie slammed his fist down on the counter. "Okay, where were you, Claudia?" he shouted.

I jumped. I had never seen him so mad before. "Don't yell at me," I said.

"Tell me where you were!" Charlie demanded.

"I was with Jody. You said it was okay," I whispered.

"No," Charlie declared. "I said it was okay for you to sleep at Jody's house."

"I did," I insisted.

"You're lying to me, Claud," Charlie said.

I just stared at him. I couldn't lie to him and say I *wasn't* lying. I didn't know what to do.

"We know you didn't sleep at Jody's," Julia told me. "Charlie called Mrs. Lynch. She thought Jody was staying here last night."

"You called Jody's mom?" I asked angrily. "So now you're checking up on me?"

"No, I wasn't," Charlie said. "But maybe in the future I should."

"Mrs. Fremont from school called Charlie at the restaurant," Bailey put in.

Uh-oh. I sank down into one of the kitchen chairs. This was going to be a *bad* conversation.

"I tried to call you at Jody's to tell you to come home," Charlie continued. "I thought we needed to talk about what's been going on. Why did you cut school all week?"

I stared down at the table. I was so tired and upset that I felt like crying. "I didn't exactly cut *all* week," I said.

"Claud! I know everything!" Charlie yelled. "The cutting, the lying. You forged my signature on a note! What's going on with you?"

"I only cut school because no one would lend me money for a ticket to the Band X concert." Now I *was* crying.

All three of them just stared at me.

"So you're saying it's *our* fault?" Bailey exploded.

I shrugged. "KZAK had a contest, where they gave away free concert tickets," I explained. "So Jody and I cut school to come here and call in and win. But we didn't win. So then we heard that Record World was giving away free tickets to the first hundred people to get there this morning. So we spent the night at the mall."

I reached for a napkin and blew my nose. I looked up at my brother. "And we got them, Charlie. We got the tickets!"

Charlie only shook his head. "I can't believe this," he said.

"I'm sorry," I said. "Really. I won't cut school anymore or stay out all night. Not ever again."

"Good." Charlie nodded.

"And from now on, I'll always let you know where I am," I continued. "I'll call you tonight, from the concert, and I'll—"

"Claudia," Charlie broke in. He was staring at me as if I had just said I found a cure for cancer. "You have got to be kidding me."

"W-what do you mean?" I asked.

"You're not going to the concert."

"What?" I cried. "Why not?"

"Because you're grounded," he said.

"But—but I said I was sorry!" I exclaimed.

"And you should be," Charlie told me. "But you still can't go to the concert."

I couldn't believe it. It wasn't possible. "You can't do this to me!" I cried. "After everything I've done this whole week to get those tickets—now you won't let me go?" My voice choked with tears. It wasn't fair!

Charlie sighed. "Don't you see, Claud? The things you did to get those tickets were wrong. That's *why* you're grounded."

"And for the scare you gave us," Julia added.

"Julia, just stay out of this," I snapped.

"Hey! Bailey and I were out all night looking for you,"

she told me. "We were scared out of our minds! We thought something awful had happened to you."

"But that has nothing to do with the concert!" I cried. "I won't stay out all night ever again. I promise. But please, *please* let me go to hear Band X!"

Charlie only shook his head. "No, Claud. You can't talk me out of this. You're grounded for the next two weeks. Period."

I didn't know what to say. I was so tired I couldn't think straight. I couldn't stop the tears running down my face. And I couldn't sit there anymore and listen to Charlie lecture me.

I stomped out of the kitchen and ran upstairs. I brought the phone into my room, crawled into bed, and called Jody.

"Jody!" I moaned when she picked up. "I got caught! Now I'm grounded! I can't go to the concert!"

"You're kidding," she said. "Wow. I can't believe it."

I told her how Julia and Bailey were out looking for me all night. And how Charlie had called the police.

"Wasn't your mother mad that you lied about sleeping over here?" I asked Jody.

"Yeah, she yelled at me. She says I'm grounded, too," Jody told me. "But by tonight, she'll forget about it."

"Not Charlie," I said. "He'll probably stay home tonight just to make sure that I don't go out."

We were both quiet for a couple of seconds.

"Um, Claud? Since you won't be using your concert ticket, do you mind if I use it?" Jody said.

"What do you mean?" I asked. "You already have a ticket."

"I know. But I can't meet Troy and Scott alone. I thought maybe I could ask somebody else in our class to come."

"Oh." I was hurt. *Really* hurt.

After all Jody and I had been through together to get those tickets! I mean, couldn't she at least have waited a couple of hours before asking to use my ticket?

"I guess it doesn't matter," I mumbled. "Take it."

"Hey, thanks, Claud. You're the best."

"Whatever."

"Well, I better be going. I've got to make some calls and then catch some z's before the concert. I'll call you tomorrow!"

"Bye," I said, and hung up.

Some people have all the luck, I thought. I bet Jody doesn't even care about seeing Band X. She only wants to see Troy.

I buried my face in my pillow. Tears stung my eyes. It was all Jody's idea to cut classes, I thought angrily. This whole thing was *her* idea, and now I'm getting in trouble!

It's not fair!

126

She should stay home with me tonight. If she was a good friend, she wouldn't go without me.

I sighed.

The truth was, I couldn't feel *too* mad at Jody. I mean, her mom didn't even seem to care that Jody stayed outside all night.

She didn't call the police.

It's too bad Jody's parents have no time for her, I thought. *My* mom and dad would have cared. *My* mom and dad would have gone out looking for me.

I thought of Charlie's furious face. He was just as worried about me as Mom and Dad would have been, I realized. He's not trying to be mean—he's only trying to teach me a lesson the way they would have.

But I was mad at Charlie.

I turned over in bed and pulled my pillow over my head.

If Mom and Dad were alive, they would have given me money for the concert. I wouldn't have had to cut school or sleep at the mall.

It was all Charlie's fault.

I'll never forgive him, I thought.

chapter fifteen

H ey, Claud?" Bailey called. "Are you awake?"

I rolled over in bed and glanced at my clock. It was eight o'clock! I must have been asleep all day, I realized.

"Claud?" Bailey called again. "We're leaving."

I didn't answer him. The last thing I wanted to do was tell Bailey and Julia to have a great time at the Band X concert!

The front door closed behind them. I heard Charlie coming upstairs. "Claud?" he called. "I've got to run out for a bit. Could you watch Owen, please?"

"Yeah," I said. I didn't want to talk to Charlie ever again. But I couldn't make Owen suffer just because Charlie was a jerk.

I opened my door and took Owen's hand. We went

down to the living room and made a whole city out of blocks. Then we knocked it down. Owen is so cute when he laughs. But even he couldn't make me forget about missing the concert.

I'd just taken Owen into the kitchen to make him something to eat when Charlie came back home. He handed me a bag.

"What's this?" I asked.

"Open it up and see, Claud. It's for you."

I opened up the bag and pulled out the new Band X CD.

"No, thank you," I said, handing it back to him. I sat at the kitchen table and pulled Owen onto my lap. I didn't want to look at Charlie. Nothing he could do would make me forgive him.

"Come on, Claud, take it," Charlie insisted. "I want you to have it."

"No. It'll just make me think of things I'd rather forget."

I kept my eyes on the CD as Charlie slipped it back into the bag. I was *dying* to put it on and listen.

"Hey, I'm angry about what you did," Charlie said. "But I got you this to let you know that I also love you. And that I understand why you did all that stuff."

"You—you do?" I asked, totally confused.

Charlie nodded. "I wasn't exactly perfect at your age," he admitted.

"Then why are you punishing me?" I asked. "It's not fair!"

"Well, it was different when Mom and Dad were alive," Charlie said.

"Why? Why does it have to be so different now?"

"Because, Claudia, if the state doesn't think I'm a fit guardian, they'll take you and Owen away." Charlie sat down next to me and gave me a serious look. "They'll send you to live with another family."

"I know," I said. I hugged Owen tighter. It was hard to be mad at Charlie when we were talking about something so important. Still, I *was* mad.

"But what does all that have to do with Band X?" I demanded.

"We had to call the police last night to help us look for you," Charlie said. "Your guidance counselor had to call me because you've been cutting school. The social workers will hear about all of this, Claud. It might make them decide that I'm not a good guardian for you and Owen."

I felt terrible.

All of a sudden, everything that Charlie was saying made total sense. How could I have been so thoughtless? Of course the police would have to tell Social Services that Charlie didn't know where I was for a whole night. And of course Social Services would check my school records.

I had risked my *family* for some dumb concert. I didn't know what to say. My eyes filled with tears. I pressed my cheek against the top of Owen's head.

"Owen sleepy," Owen said, rubbing his eyes.

"Okay, big fella." Charlie lifted him off my lap and up onto his shoulders. "I'll take you upstairs. Maybe Claudia will put on some music while I'm putting you to bed."

He winked at me. I knew what he meant—that he still wanted me to have the CD he bought me.

As I watched my brothers leave, I realized how much I loved them. I would be miserable if we ever got separated.

I wiped the tears from my eyes. I would never do anything to get us in trouble again.

By the time Charlie came back downstairs, I was listening to the fourth cut of the new Band X CD.

"This is great, Charlie," I said, punching STOP on the CD player. "You have to hear it from the beginning." I punched PLAY and the first song began again.

"How about a late supper?" Charlie asked. "Hungry?"

"I'm starving."

"Have a seat," he said. "I'll make you the biggest sandwich you've ever seen in your whole life." Charlie smiled.

And I smiled back. Then Charlie and I sat in the kitchen, eating and talking and listening to Band X. I even got my violin and played along with Jam for a while. I was sad to miss the concert. But this wasn't so bad.

I was surprised when I heard voices, and Julia and Bailey walked into the kitchen. I glanced at my watch. It was almost one o'clock in the morning!

"Anybody hungry?" Charlie asked.

"Definitely!" Bailey and Julia said at the same time.

While Charlie scrambled eggs, Julia and Bailey told me all about the concert. They remembered lots of great details about Jam. It was the next best thing to being there myself.

"It *was* a great concert," Bailey said after a while. "But I got totally soaked—the guy behind me dumped an entire Coke over my head by accident."

Julia, Charlie, and I cracked up.

"Thanks for laughing," Bailey complained. "It kind of ruined my anniversary celebration with Sarah. And I don't think this shirt will ever get clean again."

"Hey, that reminds me, Bay," Julia said. "Thanks for finally doing the wash. I got to wear my favorite shirt to the concert."

Bailey looked puzzled. "I didn't do the laundry," he said. "I thought you did it when I found all my clean clothes piled up in the basement."

"Charlie!" Julia said. "When did you do it?"

Charlie laughed and said, "Not me. I thought you two had finally decided to be mature and do it together."

"I did it," I announced.

Everyone stared at me in surprise.

"Well, I was home, like, all week," I told them. "And so were all the clothes."

Everyone just kept staring.

"Come on! It's not like you have to be a brain surgeon to figure out how the washer works."

"I'm impressed, Claud," Charlie said. "Nice work."

"Hey, Julia and I must have known it was you," Bailey said with a smile. "Right, Jules?"

Julia grinned back at him. "Right. 'Cause why else would we have chipped in to get you this?" She put her bag on the table and pulled out this amazingly cool black Band X concert T-shirt.

I held the T-shirt up against my chest.

"So, what do you think?" I asked.

"Perfect," everyone said.

I looked around at my smiling family.

"Right," I agreed. "It's absolutely perfect."